ONE SUMMER of LOVE

by

I0525923

CHARLES NUETZEL

WRITING AS "FRED MACDONALD"

The Borgo Press
An Imprint of Wildside Press

MMVII

Dedicated to all the Connies, Pats, and Davids of the world, who somehow find survival—and, maybe, love!

Copyright © 1968, 2007 by Charles Nuetzel
Originally published as *Nympho* under the pen name, Fred MacDonald

SECOND EDITION

CONTENTS

ABOUT THE AUTHOR

Charles Nuetzel was born in San Francisco in 1934, and writes:

"As long as I can remember I wanted to be a writer. It was a dream I never thought would materialize. But with the help of Forrest J Ackerman, who became my agent, I managed to finally make it into print.

"I was lucky enough not only in selling my work to publishers but also ending up packaging books for some of them, and finally becoming a 'publisher' much like those who had bought my first novels. From there it as a simple leap to editing not only a sci-fi anthology, but a line of sci-fi books for Powell Sci-Fi back in the 1960s. Throughout these active professional years I had the chance to design some covers and do graphic cover layouts for pocket books & magazines."

Much of his work in covers and graphics are a result of having had a father who was a professional commercial artist, and who did a number of covers for sci-fi magazines in the 1950s and later for pocket books—even for some of Mr. Nuetzel's books.

In retirement he has become involved in swing dancing, a long time lover of Big Band jazz. But more interestingly world travels have taken him (and his wife Brigitte) across the world, to Hawaii, Caribbean, Mexico, Kenya, Egypt, Peru, having a life-long interest in ancient civilizations. His website is full of thousands of pictures taken during these trips.

INTRODUCTION

This was a special book for me. I'm not quite certain, for sure, why it became so important. It was, after all, designed to meet certain requirement of the marketplace at the time. But, for some reason, I couldn't cheapen it up to the "lowering standards" that publishers were demanding—not in this case. I actually took a little more time with it than usual.

It was the theme that hooked me.

We all have some person in our past which lingers, haunts, and stays locked up in our memories as "unfinished business" and it stays with us for the rest of our lives.

We wonder what if things had happened differently. What might have happened if we'd made a right turn rather than a left, at a number of possible moments, events, that were turning points in the relationship.

In simple terms, there are those past relationships that never entered into intimancy for one reason or another; usually for moral or ethical or simply "by chance" being diverted from becoming acted on.

Or, perhaps, it was a raging affair where something went wrong or where the needs of one person countered with the needs of the other, and it was impossible to continue on. And things just simmered out, incomplete, leaving haunting memories to feast on in lonely moments, across the years that tended to idealize those past events into something they may never have really been.

We seldom get a second chance to fix things. Life isn't a landscape that generously offers the ability to go back in time and alter events.

But sometimes, magically, events can come up to give a person the chance not only to look back, but to finally face up to what really existed, what still exists, and get a chance to pick things up and let them become totally satisfied and completed, once and for all.

That's what *One Summer of Love* is all about.

It ended up being published under the byline of Fred MacDonald, in a somewhat shorter and different form than it is now being presented.

I have, for this expanded version of the book, returned its original title.

It is now the story I always wanted it to be. *One Summer of Love* has truly become a study of lost love, rediscovered.

—CHARLES NUETZEL
Thousand Oaks, California
July 2006

CHAPTER ONE

Dave Carter's tall, broad form was all but hidden behind the tiki-bar as he searched for the bottle of expensive Scotch that was hidden by the cheaper party booze. His head was already spinning, both from drinks and from the jarring fact that his wife's sister was now visiting them.

A good drunk might calm down the crazy erotic images that flashed through his mind every time he looked at his sister-in-law. Scotch and cream were supposed to help ulcers; so he had been told, but it wouldn't help the burning fire in his gut for Connie.

Everybody had a lost love, a person who had passed through their lives, leaving unfinished business behind to haunt them. His wife's older sister was his demon fantasy.

The years had been physically generous to Connie, what life had been like in Hollywood, they didn't know—that had always remained somewhat shaded, details avoided. Pat had said her sister was going through a difficult time. The two sisters had talked quite a bit in private during the first hours of her arrival. The details had not been shared with him. Pat never revealed any confidence. Pat was a quiet, thoughtful woman, gentle and caring. Her sister had always been more extroverted.

Connie had managed to keep a more or less safe distance from Dave, except for that momentary embrace when she entered the house.

She was a breathtaking woman, far more beautiful then when she'd left town for California, so many years ago. She was pure glamour with a polish and sophistication that hadn't been evident when they had their summer romance.

The first look at Connie had stunned him. And when she'd come warmly into his arms for a sisterly hello the feel

7

of that lush body had sparked old memories. That one, innocent seeming, momentary greeting had shaken him to the core. For just a moment she seemed to cling needily to him.

Her visit was unexpectedly jarring. The timing was very bad. All he needed was Connie lounging around the house.

At this time of his life an affair with someone, anyone, might be a logical solution to a lot of problems. And if Connie so much as batted and eyelash his way it would make things terribly awkward.

He'd never cheated on Pat—not that the idea hadn't been tempting at times. There were plenty of women who were willing to enter into casual one-night stands. The single life was hell and some marriages were much the same. Just surviving on a daily basis could be a crushing experience. Nothing was perfect. No relationship ideal.

And his marriage was going through some difficult times.

"Hey, what's you doin' down there?" a throaty female voice chanted above the churning conversational and musical blare of the party.

That voice! Ruth Milton. *Oh, god, seduction city itself!*

She was Ben's dark-haired, bouncy spouse. They lived down the street and were great party people. But very open about their views concerning sex and marriage. They had an open marriage but had never made unwanted passes at anybody. Yet the stories he'd heard about Ruth were pretty fiery! Considering his mood, she was all he needed!

Ben delighted in telling detailed, possibly extrapolated, versions of his sexual adventures, both with Ruth and other women. He never named names, but the stories were pretty racy. He went out of his way to say things like: "She'll do ya with hands, mouth and where it does her the most good! Likes doing it while watching me with another woman!" It was obvious that an arrangement could be made for a swap-party with them. Something nobody had ever come out and talked about.

Yet Ben, at parties, was innocently friendly with the women. Ruth, on the other hand, took a more aggressive

8

path—dancing with her was like having sex, standing up, with clothes on! She enjoyed brazen flirtations, even if innocently played with untouchables like himself.

He figured she got a charge creating mental fantasies in men's minds. And Ruth knew just how to package herself, and how to inspire desire without stepping over the line.

Actually, conversational gambits with her could be a lot of fun, flitting around the edges of verbal seduction without crossing a line.

"Well?" she pushed, throatily. "What's ya doin' down there?"

"Finding myself a drink," Dave laughed, a little embarrassed, much like a boy caught reaching into a cookie jar.

"With all this stuff on the bar?" Her voice was far too low; husky.

Dave found the Scotch bottle, stood. "Ulcer!"

Laughing with full lips spread wide over even teeth, she said a little too loud: "That's new, never heard of *Ulcer Scotch!*"

"No...*my* ulcer! Scotch and cream, good for the ulcer," he explained, pouring himself a stiff three fingers of the amber liquor. Dipping down behind the bar, he opened the small icebox, got cream, and then added it to the booze.

Ruth was already helping herself to a stiff shot from the bottle. "Gotta see how Ulcer Scotch tastes!"

He nodded, irritated by her depletion of his private stock; and frustrated by the low-cut of her dress that revealed a good portion of bulging flesh.

At parties she was always dressed in low-cut, tightly revealing dresses, that caught a man's eyes. Suddenly he realized he was staring down her neckline.

"Like what ya see, luv?" she laughed.

"Sorry." He felt embarrassed.

"Don't be. Nice havin' a man enjoy the sites!" Then she said more seriously: "Kinda funny how men are so taken by a woman's boobs."

He laughed, asked: "What's so funny about that? Pretty natural."

"Oh, I know that, honey. But what is it that turns you guys on?"

9

"Are you kidding?"

"No, not at all." She grinned up at him, almost seductively, certainly teasingly, said: "Well, what is it that you like?"

"Well…" he stumbled on that one.

"Come on, Dave. I'm serious. Always wondered. And I'm asking a man who…I figure is a friend in need. And I need to know."

"Yes, I can imagine what you need," he chuckled.

She reached out and gripped his arm, caressingly, while looking rather seductively into his eyes.

"You know my rep. Just ask and you'll receive!"

"Now, be a nice lady."

"I am. Nicer than you'll ever know. Sad to say," she murmured.

At that point she fell silent as if she knew the line had been drawn and stepping beyond that would be simply impolite.

Their eyes met for a moment, Ruth's hiding—far too awkwardly—amused sexual invitation. Par for the course. But it seemed as if she were saying, out loud, *I wonder what you're like in bed.*

Of course that was his imagination.

Still she seemed to be literally shredding the clothing off his body. She had never been so obvious. At least not with him.

A shiver rushed though him.

In order to escape that seething hot gaze, Dave's eyes flinted around the room then spotted Connie, through the door that led into the large playroom. She was talking to, of all people, Ruth's husband.

God, she looks beautiful, he thought, a real jab of jealousy stabbing at him. Ben would just love to make a pass at her. In fact he had said as much to Dave earlier that evening.

"Does she or doesn't she?" the man had asked.

"What?"

"Well, being in show-biz. That's a pretty wild life out there in Loony Town. And she's decked out to seduce a blank wall!"

10

"Hands off," Dave warned.

"Hell, you know me. I only make passes at willing lasses! But, she's something out of heaven—and hell combined."

"She's had a rough time of it," he suddenly confided in his friend. "Hollywood's been tough on her, I guess."

"Really? You'd never know that from the look of her. She's a super lady!"

The conversation stopped there and now he saw that Ben was being very cozy with Connie.

She knew how to take care of herself. It was never said in so many words, but he guessed she'd slept with some men here and there to get parts.

Suddenly Ben left Connie and she turned Dave's way. For a moment their eyes met.

Ruth's voice broke into his thoughts. "Your sister-in-law is quite a woman, making a real point with all the men. You knew her before you knew Pat, didn't you?" He turned, looked at Ruth. She had already consumed her first drink of Scotch and was now feeling the combined effects of that and the rum punch he'd mixed for the party.

"We knew each other," he admitted blandly. "That was twelve years ago or more. Ancient history!" He wanted to be rid of Ruth, but couldn't think of any polite way of going about it. One innocent flirtatious push and he'd ended up making a bloody fool of himself. Anything to escape thoughts of Connie.

Taking the Scotch and cream, he swallowed down half of it as Ruth said: "Isn't it wild, having her staying here?"

"Not really," Dave lied. "Just another sister-in-law story."

Ruth touched his check tenderly. All quiet sex. "You're cute, Dave." She laughed lightly, as if joking. "I've always found you such a darling. Could just eat you all up...well...if you were on the dinner table, that is."

"That's what you say to all the guys."

"Yes. Perhaps."

"You're just a naughty flirt!" he chuckled, trying hard to avoid the obvious implication of her words.

11

"Sometimes naughty, sometimes nice. You know me! I just love to flirt!"

"Yes, I've noticed. Though…sometimes it can be difficult to tell where it really is meant to lead."

She smiled mysteriously up at him, shrugged, said: "Well, there's flirt and there's flirt!"

"And the difference?" he asked.

"Well, there's the flirt that teases without any temptation to do more than that. Then there's the flirt that can lead to a cozy nicely shared bed."

"Okay. That's obvious."

"Well…I don't make passes at any ol' laddie. But it wouldn't be difficult to find you a desirable target."

That was edging just too close to a serious pass.

As if realizing how close those words had come to crossing the line, Ruth leaned back, glanced over his shoulder at Connie, then said softly: "Why do I think you're lying to yourself and to me…about your lovely sister-in-law?"

"What in the world would make you say that?" he said, defensively, almost angry.

"Well, she is one sexy package. And considering what I know about life and women and men…and all that stuff…I'll tell you she's one wild lady to have swimming around in our town, and in your house. What a beautiful hot temptation she'd be to any man alive! And so close to you!" She glanced back at him, eyes probing. "I can imagine what must be hankering in the back of your mind!"

She laughed lustily at that. "She's one hot lady!"

"Christ!" he muttered, half to himself, then to her: "She's Pat's sister, for God's sake."

"Yes. Of course, an untouchable." The wicked twinkle in her eyes added: *just like me!*

"Ancient history!" he blurted. "Nothing more!"

"If you say so," she offered, smiling knowingly. Then more seriously added: "Well, never mind that. But I've never seen you so on-edge. You look like a man on fire."

"Oh, come on, now."

"Well, okay. But I've never seen such a hungry look in a man's eyes…who wasn't on the make for some fun and games. And…honestly? You literally look…" Her voice

12

trailed off. "Never mind."

"What?"

"Just never mind. Maybe I should just step into your arms and make the most of it!" she teased, winking. "I sure know when a man's ripe for the picking, I do know that, you can bet you...well, whatever." She shrugged, looking a bit uncertain, as if she had leaped across a line beyond which she shouldn't have moved. "I'm sorry, Dave. I'm in one of those moods. And you're not the man to be playing that kind of game. Just that...the drinks, I suppose. And...well..."

The words and the expression on her face lacked conviction. But she added: "Just you seem...lost and needy. Sorry, I don't make passes at...well you know what I mean!"

"Sure."

She shrugged, and merely smiled at him.

A flush burned his cheeks. He looked away, then back at Connie. Now she was talking to Harvey Peterson, one of the bachelor-studs from the office; a man who, by reputation, would probably be making a direct pass at her body before the night was up—and he wouldn't stop at Go or collect two hundred dollars...but, maybe score. Probably not.

He kept trying to avoid Ruth's eyes. She was kind of frightening. There was no doubt that she would make a serious pass if he gave her any encouragement. He wished she'd go away.

Through the double-glass doors that led from the den to the patio, just beyond Ruth, Dave spotted his wife dancing with Ben Milton at a respectable distance. The music beat loudly from the playroom. Suddenly Dave wanted to be someplace alone and quietly get drunk.

Or in bed with Pat. Then maybe things would look different. Maybe she'd be different.

He finished off the Scotch, lay the glass on the bar, his fingers gripping it in an effort to restrain himself from the sudden urge to scream. His mind whirled with memory of how it had been with Connie.

Frantically, he attempted to shake off such thoughts. She was off-limits; had been ever since he married Pat Anderson. Yet, when his wife had called him at the office the other day to say Connie had telegrammed from Reno that she was arriving for a much-needed vacation and visit, Dave had reacted electrically.

Until that moment, he had almost managed to forget Connie. He'd actually believed it was completely over between them.

Then this afternoon, coming home early, to help with the party, meeting Connie at the door, had been like a physical blow in the stomach. All worries about the contract, the political shifting at the office, slashed away. Connie had been dressed in a tight-fitting white blouse and red shorts. The blouse was opened at the top to reveal the upper swell of her full breasts. Her legs were still flawless, the flesh tanned, smooth, sensual in the way women dreamed of, but usually never managed at any age.

He didn't want to think of Connie.

His eyes focused on his present surroundings, glanced at Ruth, then moved swiftly away. He looked at the modern painting hanging over the bar which Pat had bought for two hundred dollars last Christmas, as a present for him. It was attractive in its sweeping blue and red lines, painted on an emerald green background. The subject matter was up to the viewer to decide on—and, he believed, so was the top and bottom and side. It hung with the artist's signature upside down because the design then reminded Dave of a sailing ship making its way through a greenish fog. Very unearthly, but imaginative. He passed over the squat Buddha, which had been his present to Pat the year before and then rested on the desk where he did his nightly homework. He should be there now, doing some paper work on Hendricks contract.

Connie's voice sounded very close. and he turned in time to see her and Harvey step through the door.

David felt trapped.

14

CHAPTER TWO

"Well, hello, brother," Connie greeted. Her smile was warm. Her deep blue eyes flashed toward Ruth, as if accusing him of something very un-husbandly. It was a knowing, calculated examination of the woman, then she looked at him, once more.

Harvey had his arm around Connie's waist; his fingers were just below the curve of her swelling breasts.

David tore his eyes from her, took the bottle of Scotch and poured himself a drink.

"Hitting it hard, Dave?" Harvey accused, lightly. "Bossy wouldn't approve!"

"The hell with him! What business is it of yours?" he snapped back, not looking up.

"Hey, don't take me seriously, kid," Harvey cried, an awkward laugh attempting to accent his statement.

Ruth put in: "It's that nasty old ulcer of his. You don't want to blame Davy-boy. He's simply a doll, really."

"I didn't know about the ulcer," Connie said, concerned. "You didn't mention that."

"No need. Scotch and cream best thing." David added the cream slowly to the Scotch, keeping his eyes fixed on the glass, afraid to look up. He was shaky, hands damp with sweat. The blare of the music from the playroom blasted louder in his ears.

"How about drinks?" Harvey asked in a much too loud voice. "For me and my little girl," he added, squeezing Connie.

Everybody was getting a little drunk, now. Considering the time, well past eleven, it was not surprising. Liquor had flowed fairly fast into everybody's glass.

15

Connie reached for the Scotch bottle, which was now already half empty. David reminded himself to get another bottle at the liquor store tomorrow. He followed the movement of Connie's lovely, slender hands, and the long red nails seeming to tease him. She could be violent in the last moments of love-making. He remembered, her nails could create new peaks of pleasure.

Harvey was saying, "Dave, you really know how to give a party. Booze, dips and chips, and let the guests turn themselves on."

"The *only* way," David commented, holding his drink much too tightly. "Especially with one yanked together fast like this was."

"Yeah, you're great at that," Harvey announced. "Call up the folks and they come a-runnin' cause you're a real party giver!"

Ruth's voice was husky. "Dave's party-people. Pat and Dave can make any party go into orbit. I've always said, if you want to give a party, get a few people who know the ropes, then others who might be a little shy. The party-people will keep things going, circulating and dropping wise remarks. Ever since Ben and I moved into the neighborhood we've—"

"Wanna dance?" David suddenly blurted out, interrupting her conversation. His eyes had been fighting to keep away from Connie and now he knew it would be a losing battle if he stayed any longer in the room. Connie's neckline was too teasing, her figure too curvy, her lips too sensual. And he didn't dare look into her eyes. They were knowing, seductive pools, reaching right into the raw center of his soul. He ached to play his fingers into those long locks of velvet blonde hair, which floated over those creamy shoulders. He wanted to draw himself into her arms, pull her close, and rediscover the wonder of her passionate body. He wanted to lock deeply into her very being, surrender to the longing ache that raced through him every time she stepped into the room. He wanted to make love to her.

"Come on," he almost cursed, eyes focusing on Ruth. "Let's dance!"

"Why Dave!" Ruth cried, delighted, "I was wonder-

16

ing when you'd get around to asking me. Just about given up hope. He's such a hunk of a man, your brother-in-law!"

"Don't I know it!" Connie laughed.

Taking a swallow of the Scotch and cream, Dave moved around the bar, met Ruth as she came to him. She took his arm, squeezing it in a too friendly and intimate manner.

"I just knew," she murmured very softly, as they left the room, "the two still have the hots for one another."

"Christ!" he muttered, embarrassed and not knowing what to say.

"It's so obvious," she whispered, squeezing his arm. "Well to somebody who knows what to look at."

"Well, stop looking."

"I can't help it. She's...still haunted by you," Ruth noted.

"Christ I'm married to her sister! Connie's not that way."

"Of course she is. Every woman is. Just that some don't act on their impulses or needs or desires. Some just bottle them up tight. Some don't! And if I were you...I'd watch it! She's not the kind who'll keep her hands off if she wants something, needs something...and...well..."

His silence fed into hers. And Ruth's fingers squeezed into his arm again. Her hip brushed his.

David's temples were throbbing, he felt light-headed and knew the drinks were beginning to show their effect. All he could think of was getting away from Connie. Even the idea of dancing with Ruth seemed a welcomed escape.

In fact the idea of dancing with the woman was suddenly quite inviting. Ruth seemed to understand things and probably would be nice to him, under the circumstances. She had always been a good friend and nice lady. The fact that she was willing to have affairs with any number of men never got in the way of their friendship. Maybe she'd be just the right thing for him at this moment. Somebody who understood the problems and was sophisticated enough not to be shocked by them. That was an appealing idea. Maybe he could talk to her, get some advice. Maybe he could escape from the anguish and pain.

17

As they moved through the playroom with its large red stone fireplace, light modern furniture and stereo speakers blasting loudly to the slow beat of a Tommy Dorsey recording, Pat and Ben entered from the patio. Several couples were lounging before the fire, carrying on a noisy conversation.

Ben said with a good-natured laugh, "See, we're playing the old switcheroo! Nice party. Just taking your wife to get another drink. Everybody's left the dance floor. Too tame. Better with the Cha-Cha and Twist."

Pat smiled warmly and tapped David gently on the arm. "Now you be a good boy with our guests. Treat Ruthie properly. She's a nice lady."

He thought there was a strange pause on the last word, somehow almost avoiding the "d" in it.

God, what's wrong with you? Pat would never say such a thing like "she's a nice lay!" That wasn't Pat's style.

"I'm getting drunk," he muttered.

Ruth squeezed his arm again. Then suddenly said: "My, Dave, you're really all tensed up."

"What?"

"You're arm. So hard, like a rock!" She giggled. "Really hard. I didn't know you were that hard." Then she laughed at that. "With some men I'd ask: Are you that hard all over, honey?"

Without thinking, he said: "Maybe I am!"

"Well, now. What a delightful thought!"

"What?" he asked, absently.

"You being..." and she leaned close to his ear, saying, "You being hard all over. Want mommy to nurse you?"

"Sure, why not?" he countered, shocked by his own words, and at that same time not quite certain what he meant by them.

"Honey, if only you really wanted me to!" she said. "You're a real turn on!"

David wanted Pat, wanted to touch her, feel the warm tenderness of her soft body; know the comfortable feeling of love. Pat could be a very loving, caring human being; that's why he loved her so much.

But it was Ruth who came into his arms, pressed

18

quickly close so that their bodies could play out her ideal dancing form of sensual teasing. Only this time there seemed to be a lot more tension, a little more intensely close movement.

With Ruth it was hard to lead, because she took a firm grip of a dance tempo and would not deviate from that; and on the dance floor she could be quite hot and on the make. Up until now she had always been more tease, but suddenly he was aware of something far more driving in her mood.

He was immediately aware of the pressure of her soft breasts, the rhythmic grind of her hips as they danced playfully against him.

Her body pushed forward, finally meeting his as they gently moved to the slow music.

His already aroused sexual needs reacted quickly to the way her hips all but raped him. That thigh just slipped up against his groin, feeling the rigid hardness there, moving brazenly against it, not crudely, but with a skillful caressing action, that let him know she was aware of his arousal. The liquor and haunting memory of a long time ago with another woman all mixed together. Normally he let Ruth play out her little game, without much reaction or thought of taking her seriously. It was a polite game he acted out with Ruth but never with any intent of sexual acts. Yet it had never been quite this intense, quite this driven.

And at that moment he actually wanted to simply dive into her body. She seemed to be picking up on erotic needs.

It was as if she read something in his attitude, something which alerted her how easy it would be to get him to take her. She was making it obvious, for the first time, that she really would like to have an affair. She was, literally, making a blunt play for him, direct and open.

She was amazingly aggressive and brazenly suggestive, just with body action saying: *I know you want Connie and I'm right here and you can take me to any level you want...just let me know what that is and you have it, hands down.*

David wondered what drove Ruth to be like she was.

19

He wondered exactly how true the stories were about her. Last New Year's Eve with the stroke of twelve, Ruth had made her circle of the men at the party, then came to him. Her lips opened wide, her tongue sought the erotic intimacy of his mouth. David had not given in to her offer and Ruth merely went her happy way, not in the least bit miffed by the gentle rebuff.

Maybe something wild in her let the woman experience life without many restrictions. When given a chance, she'd grab it. If she wanted a man who showed equal interest, they simply went at it.

He felt light headed and encased in furious need, a hunger which had built up for a very long time. Any woman would do at this moment; but especially Ruth, who was so obviously a willing partner.

Suddenly, David realized that he had led her out onto the patio, whose dim lights did little to cut into the shadowy dark of night. He found himself maneuvering her to the edge of the cement, out across the lawn, around the corner of the house, onto the asphalt driveway. Darkness closed in tightly around them, the smell of roses was thick in the night air, the distant music coming from the playroom now softened into a background murmur, the moon high, a slim crescent, shining dimly on the world.

Ruth continued to press erotically near, her hips locked against his own, both her arms now around his neck, then one thigh moved between his, pressed, rubbed back and forth against a surprisingly stiff erection. The action was far more bold and direct, a no-holds-barred blunt pass.

She pulled her cheek away from his, looked up into his eyes. Those red lips were amused, but hauntingly inviting sexually offering.

"I do think you are open...now, finally," she murmured softly. "Enjoy!"

He didn't say anything to that, not verbally, anyway. But the way she looked into his eyes revealed that she could almost read his thoughts.

"My, how you *do* arrange things, don't you?" she laughed, as if innocent of her real meaning; she was mocking him. "One would think you were getting ideas." Her thigh

20

wiggled back and forth so seductively demanding. "Smart ones. Lovely one. Real hot ones. Such a hard one!"

All at once they weren't dancing, merely standing there, locked in a tight embrace, looking at each other. They were both half drunk.

The games were over. She was not flirting any more. She was playing at seduction without any holds barred.

The blood was pounding at David, the hotness burning his throat grew tight over every muscle. He remembered Connie. Remembered the New Year's Eve party and Ruth's offer of more intimacy in her kiss than he was willing to share.

Everything blurred and became wildly out of focus and before he realized what was happening, he had lowered his head, found her lips. The quick softness of her parted lips shocked David into a wild need. Her tongue greedily searched his mouth and then teased his to return the kiss.

His hand pawed her breast, then started down lower, reached a rounded full hip, and edged for more direct and intimate contact with her. Ruth stiffened all over, then grabbed his hand, and pulled it between her legs.

"Welcome," she murmured. "That's all yours, Dave!"

She reached down with her other hand boldly gathering her skirt until it was pulled up at one side, high above her waist. Black garter and tiny, net panties boldly exposed themselves. She grabbed his hand, which she lustfully slipped under black cloth, working his fingers so that they were touching moist, warm flesh.

"Yes, Dave..." she murmured. "Enjoy me!"

Once assured that he wasn't about to stop, Ruth released his hand and anxiously opened his zipper with shaking, frantic fingers. She moaned:

"God, that's big!" Then when failing to immediately reach his naked flesh, she cursed:

"Damn, get that out or I'll just die!"

Sanity choked at him. The words didn't shock him, just the reality of what was happening that shouldn't happen.

David quickly removed his hand from between her legs, gripped her wrist, pushing it back away from him.

"What are you doing?" she cried.

21

"Stopping this before it's too late!"

She stared up at him as if she'd been slapped, the expression on her face contorted between disbelief, passionate lust and fury.

"You can't stop now!" she hissed, reaching for him. "I gotta have that!"

David violently disengaged himself from Ruth and announced in a cold voice: "I'm sorry this happened, but..."

His words came to a stop when she suddenly slapped his face a stunning blow with the flat of her hand.

"You damned shit!" she spat out. "A screwing damned shit!"

"For Christ's sake, Ruth, I'm sorry, it was a mistake! Can't we leave it at that?"

"Crap! You best learn to park it or drive it! You got me so hot I could screw myself on a stick! Damn you!"

Shaking, Ruth suddenly turned, raced toward the house.

David didn't move. He was too numbed by what had happened. Never had he made a pass at any woman since being married. And there had been times. Like with his secretary. She had made it pretty obvious what she wanted him! In bed or on the floor or the sofa or desk. Any way he was willing to put it to her.

At the Christmas office party she had captured him in his private office, started making passes, hands all over the place. She was drunk, but serious.

His polite refusal had been attacked by an open blouse, a bra that unlatched in front, which did just that. His second polite refusal had stopped her and he'd ushered the girl out of the office and they had never said anything about it after that. He learned later that Harvey had scored big with her.

There had been the time when a professional prostitute was offered, when he was in San Francisco at a business conference. The girl was striking and beautiful and he was away from home. Pat would never have known. He'd been lonely and hard-up and let her come to his hotel room. The woman had been ready to give an all-night party. It was business with her and her body was lovely. But he just

22

couldn't cheat on Pat, even if she would never know. Even if with a high priced call-girl, which wasn't, exactly, having an affair.

Then another time, Pat was in the hospital for several weeks for a check-up, which turned up evidence that she was physically run-down enough to need a real good rest. Before having gone to the hospital their sex-life had been dead for several weeks; the pressure at the office had built up to the bursting point. He wanted female company and had phoned a woman he knew—a long-time married friend. They had almost had an affair once, before he dated Connie. Joan invited him over for dinner and he had a good cry on her shoulders. Her husband was out of town. After dinner and cocktails she'd left him in the living room for a few moments, saying there was something she had to do. Apparently going to the john but instead she came back into the living room, naked. She simply said: "Carl knows I have lovers. He doesn't mind because he can't keep up with me, Dave. From what you've told me, you need it, too. I've always wondered how we'd be together!"

She was in his arms and they were kissing passionately. Then sanity came only when he thought of his wife in the hospital. He simply said: "I can't, Joan. I can't cheat on Pat."

Joan had sighed then left the room, returning with a robe about her body, saying how sorry she was for having tried to seduce him. They parted friendly enough, but had never seen each other again.

Now, as he stood in his backyard, stunned by what had happened with Ruth, David felt a deeper sense of guilt and fear. If Ruth had been Connie, nothing would have stopped him.

The grind of his ulcer hurt for a moment then settled down. How long he was standing there before Pat came out, he didn't know.

"What'd you do to Ruth?" Pat's voice was edged, high pitched, and tense.

He looked at his wife, and wanted to pull her into his arms, wanted to escape the sudden confusion of his mind. But instead he merely shook his head.

23

"You did *something*!" Pat accused, her face set unemotionally. Those fine, even features framed in the short off-blonde hair were stubborn.

"Hell, nothing happened that—"

"She came in crying, said she was going home. Ben tried to find out what was wrong. She just...said nothing, just that something you said—Ben wanted to go out and talk to you—but Ruth made a scene. Oh, how *could* you?"

"Nothing happened," David lied. Then all at once he blurted out: "It didn't mean anything. You know how she is with the men—I wanted to teach her a lesson. And well, I guess I'm a little drunk—I kissed her, and things got a little out of hand—I was confused, didn't really know what had happened by then—thought it was you, I guess. Anyway, I stopped it, that's all."

Pat's hands went to her slender hips. Fury burned in those gray-blue eyes. "That's *all?* Oh, for God's sake, Dave!" She sounded sick, her voice shook. The look in her eyes told David all too well that there would be no communication with her tonight. Nothing!

Pat was the kind of woman who, when mad, would get quiet, and there was no way to cut through the silence until she had convinced herself that enough time had passed to cool down.

"Pat, hell! I didn't mean anything other than to stop her!" He knew this was part lie; but it was an honest one. Ruth wasn't his type. It was Connie he wanted. Then it might have been a different story all around.

Pat turned, went into the house without saying another word.

24

CHAPTER THREE

It was some time before David returned to the house. By then the place was deserted. The others had left, including Connie. He found Pat in the kitchen arranging the glasses and dishes for a morning cleaning.

He stood staring at her, trying to think of some way to make her understand. She looked very attractive when she was angry. Maybe the attractiveness was accented by the fact that she became untouchable at such times. She moved with short, jerking motions, her slender hands whipping glasses, cups, dishes from one place to another, with automatic design. The short off-blonde hair was cut just below her ears. The soft white throat teased David. Her lips were set firm lines, hiding their more shapely form. Once she turned, eyes snapped at him, then dismissed him.

"Pat, it was nothing, believe me."

"I don't want to talk about it."

"We can't leave it at this. I want you to understand that—"

She whipped around, her eyes now fiery cold. "I said I don't want to talk about it. Do you understand?"

They stared at each other for a long time, then finally she turned and continued arranging the last of the glasses.

He watched until she was finished. As Pat started past him, David grabbed for her.

She was like stone as he pulled her into his arms. A desperate need drove him to attempt the impossible. His lips tried to kiss hers, but there was no response.

"Do you mind? I want to go to bed," she announced in a low even voice; ice cold.

David released her, then waited until she had gone to

25

the bedroom. Then he went to the den, poured himself a stiff drink and sat in front of the bar, looking at the three fingers of straight Scotch.

A few moments later he had consumed half the Scotch in his glass, and begun to feel a sense of cool detachment. Everything seemed dream-like, faraway, without reality. His passes at Ruth Milton and the aftermath of it faded from his thoughts. Instead he was idly thinking about Connie, wondering where she was. Probably with Harvey. The idea of Connie and Harvey irritated David to distraction.

It was all very ridiculous, actually. Connie had walked out of his life over ten years before. There had been no formal goodbye. Just all at once, she was gone.

He had wanted to marry her, and when they'd talked about that she had simply said if things were different, she might gladly marry him. But Connie wanted more out of life than being a wife, having a bunch of kids. She wanted to see the world, become an actress and not be trapped in an unimportant town, doing unimportant things. She had always called the town Small Town, USA. Then she'd simply disappeared into Hollywoodland.

David hardly knew the woman that existed now. There had been only a couple of hours before the party. The light conversation had gone nowhere, revealed less. Connie had never made it, other than a few short parts in unimportant "B" movies and television shows, a couple of tours as a singer with small combos and a marriage that went boom after three years. She looked tired when she talked about her past life but brightened quickly after a quick after-dinner drink.

He realized that their affair never really burned itself out—merely been chopped to an end because of the Hollywood dream.

They had met in high school, but not dated until after his first semester in college, where he'd learned about sex with a number of one-night stands and a few short affairs.

That summer, when he had come home, he had bumped into Connie at the drug store, got to talking to her and on impulse asked for a date. She'd been so popular in school, becoming the senior class queen—in every way—

26

that it was amazing how easily she'd accepted him as an escort for dinner and a movie. Yet he'd had his old morality that blinded him to Connie's sexual needs; she was a hometown girl, to be protected; not violated. He hadn't read the signals right. He didn't think of Connie in the same way he thought of the girls in college.

But that first kiss on their first date blew his mind. Just the touch of her full lips gave him a quick erection. When her tongue eagerly sought entrance into his mouth, it was all he could do to control his natural impulse to make direct and fancy passes. That first night he'd managed to keep his hands off the swells of her breasts, where they pressed so tight against a red sweater.

They dated twice more, each time ending up in a necking session in his car, burning their passions right up to the point of no return before he'd somehow found the strength to bring a stop to things, short of petting. Though the third date he'd found it impossible to keep his hands off her breasts. Connie hadn't even made a polite effort to block the pass but had actually surged up against his hand. There it hadn't gone much further.

The fourth date Connie restrained him from pulling her into his arms, as had become the natural course of action after parking outside her home. She'd told him straight out: "I don't want to go through that kind of thing again, Dave! It's too much!"

Like a damned stupid kid he'd blurted out:

"What's wrong?"

Looking him straight in the eye, Connie had quite bluntly stated: "We're too mature to play around. If that's all you want, get another girl friend—not me."

It still embarrassed him to recall his reply to that blatantly open offer to either go all the way with her or completely stop. But he felt protective of a hometown girl.

In a shaken voice, he'd said: "I thought you liked necking!"

Connie had slowly shaken her head from side to side, while raising her hands to his face, placing one palm on each cheek; gentle, sensual. "I like it too much to stop. If you want the same thing I do, why should we kid ourselves?"

27

That was Connie, direct to the point and not about to be taken too seriously.

He'd never experienced anything so good before Connie. Sexually, she was about the best thing a man could have. Emotionally it was a shattering experience, because she didn't want anything serious to develop between them.

They actually went to a motel out of town that first time. He couldn't believe how wonderful Connie was. It turned into a mind-blowing experience. The moment they'd gotten into the room they started touching, caressing, almost tearing one another's clothing off, landing on the bed, stark naked and devouring one another in such wild abandon that they were left exhausted in the aftermath of that first union. It was a blur of sensations and he never did, really, remember the details. It was a stunning experience.

They were both shaken. Their bodies had become soaked with lover's sweat. Suddenly he knew that the feeling he felt was far more than sexual. With that he accepted a total sense of love.

Looking at her beautiful body, David became overwhelmed with feelings he'd never known were in him.

"God, that was something...beautiful!" he had almost moaned, shaking, on the verge of saying something else, but not quite sure what that might be. The words were bubbling in the back of his brain, bursting to be recognized.

"I know, Dave," she murmured softly. "It *is* something...nice. Quite nice."

He faced her, fairly gasped at the raw desire that consumed him. Those breasts had been wonderful to fondle, to kiss. Now he felt the erotic need all but overwhelm him.

"Let's get married," he blurted out, suddenly realizing that he really loved her.

"It's not necessary, Dave," she told him in an even, slightly wistful voice.

"What does that mean?" But he knew.

"Let's not play word-games, Dave." She gazed honestly into his eyes. It was unnerving.

"I love you, Connie. Maybe I've always loved you! Just didn't know what love was."

"Sexual desire isn't the same thing, Dave." She put

28

out her cigarette, leaned closer. "I'm hot and hungry for you! Sex hungry."

These words coming from Connie Anderson seemed startlingly out of place. He had known her from a distance through high school, seen her mature from a highly attractive young teenage girl into a striking young woman.

He laughed, more nervous and embarrassed than anything else. "I guess you're right."

Then he added: "But there's more to it, Connie, than that."

She shrugged. "Why complicate things more than necessary? Obviously we both...well, have orgasmic feelings for each other. Why not leave it that way? I don't want to get married, Dave. That much I want you to understand. It's not you. It's just that I'm not planning on anything quite that serious. Not right now. You understand, don't you?"

David considered her words, then said: "I guess so...I couldn't afford getting married right now. It was foolish—"

She leaned closer. "No, Dave. It's not foolish to tell a woman you love her and that you want to marry her—but it would be foolish to call things off, just because wedding bells aren't about to ring. I *do* love you, Dave. But I mean mostly in an orgasmic way. I knew this from the first date. I desperately wanted to have sex. I'm a passionate woman and don't go out with a man I couldn't climb into bed with— willingly! That's blunt, but honest. Crudely put, Dave, I like sex a lot. I really want you."

She slipped hotly into his arms. The kiss was overwhelming, taking into play all parts of their bodies. She was pressing up against him, greedily, hips and thighs active. When they broke from the kiss, Connie laughed huskily.

"You know, I want you, right now!" She grabbed playfully between his legs. She laughed happily while tenderly fondling him with both hands.

Then they made love, wildly and passionately.

The next night they returned to the same motel. After he had mixed drinks in the bathroom, he rejoined Connie to find that she was lying in bed, the covers pulled tight around her curving body.

It was the first time he remembered her in that way;

29

yet it was the most powerful and vivid memory of Connie. She was always naked under the bed-sheets, waiting for him.

The rounded swell of her hips and the mounds of her breasts under the green covers created a catch of pleasure to surge through him. For a moment he stood there at the foot of the bed, holding the glasses in each hand, just staring down at her. That long blonde hair floating around her head, down over the point of her shoulders, like silken waves.

"You are beautiful," he breathed out in a soft whisper.

"You look pretty good yourself. Six feet of attractive hard muscle. I love touching you. Feeling your muscles, your body." Her arms reached up to him. "Come over here, lover. I can't wait another moment to have that big, bursting pile driver touching my flesh."

He had a struggle to keep from spilling the drinks as he set the glasses on the nightstand.

"The lights," she laughed, when he started to lean over her.

"To hell with the lights!" He moved onto the bed, pulled down the blankets so that her large breasts were exposed, the pink nipples like lovely roses tipping supple creamy mounds.

"Aren't you going to get undressed?" she teased, gently pushing him away. "After all, you have me at a disadvantage."

And it didn't take him long to strip and come into her arms. It seemed as if they never stopped making love and never would stop wanting to and would be together forever.

By the end of summer, Dave had attempted every means he knew to convince Connie to marry him. In the end she admitted she loved him, but said she needed to get out of the town, become an actress. They would write one another. But no letters came to him in the following months and David never had the strength to write Connie. By the end of the year he did receive one short letter saying she was in Hollywood, had an agent and was working for a small band as a singer. That was the last personal communication he had from her.

By the time he finished college and returned home,

30

getting a job at the firm where he now worked, his memory of Connie was more a distant longing, but no longer hurt. There had been a couple of serious-type of romances at college, which fizzled out for one reason or another. They had helped him to forget Connie. Then one evening, when he went to a liquor store for some beer, he saw Pat, Connie's younger sister, who worked there as a clerk. At first he didn't recognize her. It was Pat who brought attention to herself. "Aren't you Dave Carter?"

"You're Connie's sister, aren't you? How is she?"

"Fine. Engaged to some producer out in Hollywood," Pat had said quickly.

Nothing more than casual conversation followed, then he had left. But the next time he went to get beer, he was disappointed by the fact that Pat wasn't working that day. The next day, having learned when she worked, he went to the store and before realizing what he was doing, asked her out on a date, which was readily accepted. Their dating was casual enough at first, then became a steady thing. A little more than a year later he proposed. She accepted, but set the date for their marriage for six months later. An affair began immediately after their engagement, and she became pregnant two months before the marriage date. They married immediately, disappointing both sets of parents. Life after that developed into a natural pattern. Pat was a good wife and excellent mother. Their life together had been extremely happy during the first years. Their marriage was nice, at times very romantic, at others rather placid and sometimes, like now, somewhat rocky.

David's thoughts snapped back to the present. The glass in his hands was empty. He took a bottle of whiskey and poured a strong drink. He was drinking far too much. Lately, boozing had become a habit; but there were pressures surging in around his life, both privately and professionally.

Going out into the playroom, he sat on the long, low white sofa and stared into the dying coals in the fireplace. He tried to blot out the thoughts about Connie and about Pat.

Automatically work problems focused in his mind, slashing all sexual thoughts into thin air.

He'd been given a big hairy problem a couple of

weeks before, when Frank Nathan took over as office manager. The assignment was horny, because it involved doing business with a woman who had a reputation of using her body to put across deals—*her* way!

It was a cute trick of Frank Nathan's. They'd never gotten along well with one another and this was Frank's way of possibly getting rid of David. Office politics was a nasty part of the business, and if you couldn't survive that you ended up on the street, unemployed.

Frank was something of a stuffed shirt, didn't drink and didn't smoke. He also didn't approve of David's habit of having a couple of double Scotches at lunch. "Work and business don't mix with liquor!" had been his only remark. Things were beginning to get a little stuffy at the office, with Frank staring down David's back, just waiting for one major mistake to make it possible to disqualify him for a promotion. Frank had another man picked for the assistant manager job: Gordon Larson, a young, intelligent snob-type. They made a cute pair. If Frank Nathan had his way, Gordon would be moving up. The only thing that kept this from automatically happening was the fact David had been promised the job by John Calvin Barton, president and owner of Barton Enterprises. But even JB would be moved to reconsider his promise if the new manager recommended against the promotions, with *facts* to back him up! Thus the Hendricks job had been thrown David's way. It was an obvious trap. And not a win-win for him, no matter what he did. Unless he could pull some rabbit out of the hat.

Everything depended on how he handled this hot assignment. *Hot* in every way!

Freda Hendricks was considered one of the most difficult business executives to deal with. She was smart, a lawyer and top executive in her firm and known to use every method and weapon at her disposal to get excellent deals for her company. Freda didn't stop short of sleeping with a man in order to get his cooperation. She was a *hot* sex-potato, for if a good deal wasn't made, Frank would claim David had been seduced into cooperating with Freda; something that would not only hurt David at the company, but damage his personal life.

32

David swallowed down hard on the whiskey, drinking as if it were water, then half staggered to the den bar, refilled his glass, returned to the sofa.

If I wanted to cheat it wouldn't be with Freda! he thought. *When sorrows come, they attack in swarms!*

All he needed was Connie Lewis coming into his life to complicate things. There were enough problems without his personal life getting more knotted up in sexual distractions.

He was finishing off the last of his drink when the front door opened quietly, then closed.

Footsteps sounded in the hallway.

He turned to see Connie tiptoe past the playroom door. She saw him, hesitated, then stopped. "What are you doing up so late?"

"Pat...she won't talk to me." Only with effort was he able to speak without slurring his words.

Connie stepped into the room, came over to the sofa, sat down. "Oh, that thing with...what's her name? Yes. Ruth. I wouldn't take it too seriously. She stood up for you pretty good."

David felt suddenly cheap and guilty. He wanted to talk to Connie, tell her what had happened and why. He said nothing.

"Don't you think you should go to bed?" Connie inquired, after a long silence.

"No. Pat wouldn't let me sleep in the same bed with her, not *tonight!*"

He found it difficult to keep from reaching out and pulling Connie into his arms. He remembered Harvey and felt the stab at his stomach. Sudden anger burned alive; hot seething jealousy.

"What were you doing out—"

"Oh, Harv invited me up for a drink. That's all." She avoided his eyes.

"Screw him?" It was a nasty remark and he felt immediately sorry for having said it.

"Dave. What's with you?" She didn't look into his eyes. "That's none of your business." Then more quietly. "Actually, no. He tried. It just didn't seem...well, right. I've

33

changed a *little!"*

She laughed at that. "We all grow up a little, don't we? Life can be a rotter at times."

David felt wild relief. He relaxed, the tension drained out of his body as if made of melting lead. Suddenly they were almost just old friends, almost comfortable with one another. "I was thinking about us, Connie. You know...during the college days."

"Oh?"

"About that summer."

"I thought you'd forgotten all *that,* by now." She kept staring into the fireplace, her hands clasped on her lap.

"One never forgets their first real love affair," David whispered half to himself.

"No, I guess not. But...after all these years, I guess you got a good laugh out of it." She sounded soft and yielding—emotionally shaken.

"Hardly. It wasn't very laughable, you know."

She now turned on him, said: "We were young and foolish—just kids trying to play adult."

"I don't think so—but that's a long time ago. Maybe I don't remember too well, after all." He nervously stood, started for the den.

"Where're you going?" She sounded alarmed.

"To get drunk."

"Don't you think you should stop?"

He turned toward her. She was standing, staring at him with deep concern etched on her lovely face. She had become much more beautiful than he remembered. Her slightly upswept nose seemed delicate against the high cheekbones and pouty lips. Large, deep blue eyes gave the appearance of innocence, while at the same time smoldering with maturity and understanding about the hardness of life. Connie was the kind of woman who did not age, but actually became more attractive as years put sensual maturity onto her body. More filled out than he remembered, more soft and voluptuous. More to make love to.

It wasn't as if the years had turned back, but rather as if nothing but their age had changed. He wondered if he had ever fallen out of love with Connie. The idea was fantastic!

34

The inner passion for her was still there inside him, raging.

Panic drove him into the den. He shakily poured a drink, then was downing it as Connie came up to him. She reached out a restraining hand, pulling the glass from his mouth. The softness of her touch all but drove David over the line.

"You shouldn't, Dave," she warned, softly.

That physical contact was all he needed.

Sanity suddenly stripped away, leaving nothing but raw nerves, need and longing to take over. Reality had spun of existence. Nothing existed except Connie and him. Just the need to become one with her.

David reached for her, forcefully yanked that body close. Then he was kissing her face, lips, cheek and neck with a frantic desperation; painful need.

How he wanted her! Nothing mattered any more. Only his driving need to have this woman he had loved for so long, wanted for so long.

Time had crushed out of existence. They were just David and Connie, two people who craved one another with such unlimited passion that it hurt deep down to the very core of his soul. All he could feel was the desperate need to escape into the warmth of this wonderful creature, this goddess of love.

Connie didn't respond at first; then when his mouth came around to hers again, she stiffened, her lips trembled, parted. Then abruptly she became rigid, and without warning her hands forced him away.

"We better forget that. Call it the drinks, Dave." Her voice had the same sharp edge that Pat's would have under the same kind of circumstances; but there was a longing in her eyes. Literally a desperate plea for him to stop. When he started to move close, she warned sharply: "Don't, Dave, please. You don't know what you're doing. There are things about me you don't know. I couldn't stand...the hurt it would cause—cause Pat...you...me." Then moving away, she added: "We're all tired—and been drinking too much. Come on, I'll take you to bed."

"Forget it, Connie. I'm getting drunk, and don't give a damn!"

35

He gulped down the drink, and then poured himself another. At that point the liquor slammed at him, and for a moment he swayed dizzily. The world spun, everything was pulled out of focus, became distant. Sound reverberated around the room; it was Connie's voice, he knew that much, but could not make out the words.

Movement followed, and he felt as if he were on a ship in the middle of the ocean. It wasn't until he was standing in front of the guestroom bed that David realized what had happened. Connie was supporting his body with hers, directing his moves.

"Come on, Dave," she soothed, "in you go!"

With expert care she led him to the bed, gently helped him down onto it.

A moment later he heard his voice saying, "I love you, damn it, I love you..." Then black ebbed around his thoughts and reality stopped existing.

36

CHAPTER FOUR

Connie got out of her car, locked the door, and then looked up at the tall building to her right. Nine floors, she guessed. Big for such a square Small Town, USA.

The hot sun brightly blazed its reflection in the almost solid glass walls of the *New Carver Building,* for a moment blinding her. That was where David worked.

She turned hurriedly away and her gaze fell on the cocktail lounge across the street. The sign, *Bernie's Cove,* brought distant memories into sharp, painful focus. All too many evenings she had spent there with David.

As if drawn by some invisible force, Connie made her way across the street, stepped into the dim confines of *Bernie's Cove,* moved to the bar. Pulling out a cigarette, she used the lighter Larry had given her as a present two years ago.

Connie attempted to remember what it had been like to live in this town, where nobody did anything other than slowly exist on hard work, children and screwing. Then going to church on Sundays to get a spiritual bath, so they could, for the rest of the week, screw each other and each other's mates! To say nothing about the screwing in business deals. It was all the same all over the world. But here it was petty and small town, middle class nothing.

She couldn't remember how it felt. Too much had happened in the last years. It blurred all memory of life here in the town where she was born. Only memories of David were clear and sharp. And she longed for that lost summer, the lover who had been so tender and kind and very much in love with her; but in a way that other men since then were unable to love.

37

Show business attracted a different breed of animal. Men always on the grab for a quick lay or a prolonged sex thing with some woman they could turn to as a channel for their own orgasmic frustrations.

And it wasn't nice, either, at times.

Men could be beasts. They took you to their apartment, started working a hand into your bra, drunkenly pawing their way up your legs, saying something like: "Where's that screwin' cunt, baby!"

It wasn't that Connie didn't know all the dirty little words. She'd learned most of them in Small Town, USA!

Then, there were the casting directors, the agents, the producers, and the *assistant-everybody* who were out to get themselves some hot piece! One guy wanted her to expose herself so he could simply look and fondle and finger her. How men delighted in treating a woman like some kind of meat. At times she had been turned-off so much that it was impossible to even think being with a man.

Then the women; but, oh, the women! They not only talked dirtier than men but there were the Lesbians who could get her a part, if she'd only give them a good time.

Her first Lesbian affair had been startling because her bisexual roommate was smart enough to have a dildo and knew how to use it! How strange—and even wonderful— that first experience had been! Partly because she was drunk. Mostly because of the surprise of discovering the woman had something like that—and was so willing to use it.

But it was the young male actors who proved most annoying. They were desperate to get *the* break. And it really was hell waiting endlessly for a phone call from your agent saying you had an interview—maybe a part. These men's lives were too wrapped up in *the* Career, *Ego,* and dreams of glory to know how to share themselves completely with another human being.

Refocusing on the present, Connie ordered a Dry Martini, then studied her immediate surroundings in an effort to draw the depression of Hollywood out of her thoughts. Those memories held an endless series of sexual perversions that had become so much a part of her early years in that Sin Town,

38

The walls were dark, the furnishing Early American in style. Behind the barstool, set back enough to allow a passageway, was a row of booths lining the wall; high backed darkly cushioned in brown leather.

Not much had changed in the last eleven years. But then, nothing had really changed in this town since the turn of the century. Oh, there were a few new, more modern buildings. A little more gloss here and there, maybe a bit of sophistication brought on by the very elements of the modern world. Few places on the map had been untouched by the tendrils of mass media. Then there was the so-called *new* morality, which was nothing more than a realization of what had been going on already and a willingness to admit it. Each generation had to discover its own set of rules and concepts about sex and love.

She trembled inwardly, remembering David's kiss the night before. It had been hell to shove him off. She needed a real lover! Life had cut hard scars through her. David had ripped some of the more important tender ones wide open! That had been a shock.

The Martini came and she sipped it slowly. Her eyes once more made a survey of the room. There was the jukebox, sitting at the far corner, opposite the entrance, just a little more modern but where it had always been. The back corner booth attracted her eye. It was there that she had seen David for the last time, just before he took the train back to college.

She wondered if there had been anything he might have done or said then to have killed her Hollywood dreams and caused her to marry him.

Probably not. David had tried hard enough to marry her. It was all too ironic that he was now her brother-in-law. That was a blow, which still shook her up. She hadn't even known David was dating Pat. The day the telegram came about their abrupt marriage turned gray and bleak. There was a party planned at the apartment she shared with another young actress, the one who was willing to climb into bed with either men or women.

For the first time in her life Connie became stoned to the point where memory blacked out completely. In the years before then, Connie had learned how to hold down a pretty good supply of liquor without showing any ill effects. She was supposed to be engaged to a producer but the engagement really meant a casual form of mistress.

When she woke up in a strange motel with a man she hardly knew, naked in bed, Connie realized just how much David meant to her.

The man's lips on her breasts had brought awareness into sharp focus. After that they literally ravished one another.

Only in the aftermath of that prolonged session had Connie admitted how much she had loved David. But it was too late to throw stones. The decision had been her own. The results were her punishment for being a damned stupid fool.

Life then took on a certain rhythm and sexual pattern. It was almost as if she couldn't get enough men. There were several producers and several musicians and actors who passed through her life. Some were casual affairs, some more involved—twice she moved in with a man for a long period of time; but with no hopes or illusions that anything more would develop out of it than the role of mistress.

It was all part of the game of making a living—of surviving in the world of show business.

Connie learned quickly, after coming to Hollywood, that a girl neither flatly turned down a man's passes nor casually slept around. But there were all too many times when it didn't matter, when her personal need and hungers, the nagging loneliness, the raging frustrations made it impossible to be intelligent about with whom she climbed into bed.

The old belief that you had to sleep your way to the top was standard legend without any real support in the actual film world. Sure, there were lots of men who grabbed a young piece of ass, taking advantage of innocent girls who still believed this was the way to success. But it wasn't.

A girl played the game like any woman played it in life. If she was smart enough to realize the truth.

When a man came along who was physically attractive and he wanted to sleep with her and she felt the same way, an affair grew naturally out of the relationship. It could happen on the first date or the tenth. One just didn't use up

40

their time running around with male stud-artists who were nothing but duds, professionally.

The secret of getting ahead in show business was realizing that the men who had any kind of power to help you along the way could be just as attractive as those who could do nothing. In fact, the only guy who really helped Connie get her first struggling start had never once made a pass.

If she had become a star, Hollywood would have found good reason to whisper loudly how she screwed her way to the top, but it would not have been a true or honest picture of her private life.

Not the one *she* called her personal private life.

Forgetting all the men who had shared a bed with her—she'd usually picked her lovers with the natural care of a woman who likes sex but isn't a tramp, either.

Her problem had come out of the desperate hunger for true love that was always in conflict with the other frantic hunger to make it Big. That, mixed with the lonely times, the frightening moments, had caused Connie to do some terribly disgusting things. The loneliness was crushing; a terrible agony that hung over a person night and day, reaching into their soul like an evil, dark shadow, blinding one of every emotion other than self-hate. The times when one had nobody to cuddle up to, when one was desperately needy. Long, endless periods that never really stopped. Those empty feelings lingered over even the good times, darkening them, shading them, perverting their offering joy.

And she had done a lot of things she wasn't proud of in order to escape the terrible pain. Slept with some real pigs that promised small parts in their films or a gig at their club. Men were all hands on butt, breasts and anywhere else they could get away with a free feel or total possession.

Connie realized that a woman wanting real love needed to find it outside of show-biz. All her love affairs turned sour because men wanted their egos stroked and lived a total life dedicated to love of themselves. They didn't have room to love a woman selflessly. But she was always searching for true, unselfish love. Actors and power players were always takers, not givers.

Her marriage had been a desperate and foolish at-

41

tempt to compromise; to adjust to the apparent reality of the world, in which she lived and circulated. And it happened when she was truly at a low point emotionally and career-wise.

Poor, poor Larry, she thought. She had been working as a secretary for Mr. Lewis. Her boss began making with late-hour passes, which she blocked. Larry was eight years older, a fairly good looking type, who had been married once, divorced and now lonely to have another wife. She was down and out of the picture, as far as show business people were concerned. The hard knocks had bruised her, too much. Jobs came too many times with bedroom demands—and when an affair broke off, so did all contacts controlled by the stud. She was tired of the fight, then. At the time Connie was licking those wounds and Larry's marriage proposal sounded like an easy escape. And there was always the hope that some parts might come along without strings, once she was Mrs. Lewis. It was a mistake from the beginning. Only in the last six months had she realized the truth. Larry was all most women might ask of a husband. The only thing wrong was she didn't love him and, in so many ways, the sex side had been something rather sad. He tried hard, but just wasn't much of a lover. And he could hardly keep up with a woman who had her kind of keen, voluptuous need for a lot of sex and loving.

Then, there were many chances for her to have a young stud, some of which she'd helplessly taken in a desperate attempt to make things work in the marriage. She figured what Larry didn't know wouldn't hurt him, and in fact might make things work out okay.

One man who had been hired to drive her around made it obvious he was quite interested in her. One night, when her husband was out of town, Connie had stripped naked, gone to the guest house, where the man was staying, used the extra key, and ended up slipping into bed next to him.

He was great, but she had actually felt guilty about cheating.

The next day Connie had formally fired the man, giving him a two-month paycheck and recommendations.

42

Though some six months later she'd seen him in Hollywood and they had gone to a motel and spent the day together. That was the last time she ever had any contact with him. Though there had been a few other guys.

The guilt from cheating had, in the end, been partly responsible for her deciding on divorce. It hadn't been fair to either of them.

Marriage created out of desperation and loneliness and without love—coupled with illicit sex on the side— usually either ruined itself naturally or the two people involved.

Thus Reno, and now "home." Pat was the only relative left. Their parents had died some years before in an auto accident. Somehow she'd managed to miss their funeral.

Connie finished off the Martini and then ordered another.

She considered why she had come to town alone. Pat believed she was on a shopping spree; but that wasn't true! Shopping was the last thing Connie had in mind. It was David she wanted to see. Pat had offered to go along, but Connie insisted she wished to be alone.

She felt a pang of guilt.

Yet what was wrong with wanting to talk to your brother-in-law?

Nothing. If the brother-in-law wasn't a past lover.

Nothing. If only she didn't know how easy it would be to fall into an affair with him—if David pushed just slightly!

While finishing off the second Martini, Connie opened her purse. No change there. She impulsive stood, went to the bartender, asked for change and then went to the phone booth in the corner near the entrance. She hesitated for only a moment, then taking a deep breath, dialed the *Barton Enterprises* phone number.

After going through the switchboard operator, getting David Carter's office, she felt nervous guilt. She was about to hang up when David's voice sounded over the line.

"Yes, Carter speaking."

Hesitating, Connie felt her breath catch, her breasts lunged hard against the tight bra; hot and suddenly aching.

43

"Hello, are you there?" David inquired.

Taking a deep breath, she said: "Yes, Dave, this is Connie."

It was all she could get out. And it was too late to back off, now.

Stone silence answered her. Finally, after what seemed at least a full minute, he said: "Yes, Connie."

His voice caressed her name with a deep loving tenderness. It was almost like verbal embrace.

"Dave, I'm...over at *Bernie's*...been shopping, got hungry, and...well, thought maybe it might be fun having lunch with you. My treat." She was talking too fast, too nervously. "You know...since you're just across the street it seemed silly for both of us to lunch alone and—"

"I can't get away for another hour, Connie. Wait for me. Please? I'll come as soon as I can." His voice sounded suddenly husky.

Connie hung up the receiver without saying good-bye. She was shaking. Tears clouded her vision. Hot depression flashed through her, to be replaced by extreme joy, only to digress again. It was evil what she was doing. Connie knew this. Yet she had no plans on ever letting anything happen. She simply wanted to be near him for a while. Just to talk, nothing more. She needed a friend and they had been very close so many years ago.

How stupid! It is playing with fire.

Yet the two of them had to set all that aside and try to come to some reasonable, adult understanding. It was normal for them to still have feelings for one another, but also normal to simply set them aside.

Was that possible? It had to be. It was necessary to draw some realistic lines.

She tried to convince herself that talking to David was a necessary bit of business, which simply had to be dealt with before something was misunderstood. But guilt undermined her thoughts, for she really still felt the hot fiery burn of memories in his arms. That summer had been the only real romantic relationship she ever experienced.

For some time she stood in the phone booth trying to gain control of her emotions. She told herself there was noth-

44

ing wrong with having lunch with her brother-in-law. She had every right.

In fact, Connie argued bitterly, *I have rights, too.*

David had been hers, first! He still would be hers, if things had been different. She didn't know for sure if he still wasn't hers for the taking.

Last night in his drunken state of half-consciousness, David's cry of love had haunted Connie. Sleep had come only in spurts. Of course, she had told herself, David might have meant Pat; been confused; but she doubted it.

Connie was still fighting with guilt as she returned to the bar. Taking her drink, she decided to ignore ethics. The world was a damned rotten place, a savage fighting field where everybody was on their own, sink or swim. You fought to keep alive to survive. If you were smart enough you realized the ground rules were harsh:

Win any way you can, because it's life you are fighting for; fight fair and you could be battered dead. Fight dirty, "screw-you" dirty, you might win.

She finished off the Martini and then toyed with the glass. Considered having another, then decided to hold off. She wanted to be reasonably sober when she saw David.

I have to set things right, draw a hard line, so neither of us crosses it. For Pat's sake. For their sake.

After paying for the drinks, Connie walked outside. It took her a moment to get used to the bright sunlight. Then she moved toward the department store at the corner. All the time she was telling herself nothing would ever happen between David and herself. Neither of them could do that to Pat. Yet the longing to experience the lovely abandon happiness of youth with *her* David was impossible to deny. She had a right to desire anybody in the world but not to take another woman's husband; at least not her sister's.

The more she walked, the more Connie was able to convince herself how she would simply have lunch with David. A natural event. Because he was a man and she needed a man's point of view—a man's silent understanding.

They simply had to define their new relationship of as in-laws—not past lovers. That had to be settled once and for all, in so many words, if necessary.

45

Connie went into the department store, aimlessly wandered around, and found herself standing in front of a counter fingering a lacy pink negligee. It was the kind of material men liked to see on a woman because so little could be concealed by its sheer netting.

She remembered she had never worn a negligee for David. Their inexperience in affairs, her own embarrassment at the time about going to a store and buying herself such a nightgown, had all played their parts to deny him such a moment.

She was always naked under the covers, waiting for his caresses.

Connie shook away memories, turned to leave. A saleslady stepped up.

"Can I help you?" The face was friendly but there was a hard coldness in the voice.

Connie remembered that one didn't go into a store and start picking things up without the idea of buying. Not in this town. In Hollywood, New York, San Francisco, Chicago, it was something else. But here in Small Town, USA, the rules were different.

"Oh, yes. I'll take this," Connie quickly stated. "How much?"

"Fifty-nine, ninety-nine, plus tax; Do you want me to wrap it?"

"Why not have truth in pricing? That's $60 plus tax!" she stated, a little annoyed.

"I don't do the pricing, lady. I just work here!" the woman stated, coldly. "Do you want it gift wrapped?"

"No, just a bag. For myself."

The woman eyed Connie with sudden disapproval. She was the prude-type of female men never gave a second look at. Probably never had bought such a nightgown—or if she had, wore it only in secret. The beady eyes, the long hawk nose, the firm, thin lips, coupled with that skinny flat form, would make such lacy material a perversion.

She started to ask if they would accept a check, then remembered nobody knew her in this town any more. She took three tens from her purse, handed them to the gnarled hand, held out like a greedy claw.

46

The moment the woman handed her the package, Connie rushed out, almost on the edge of panic, and not knowing why.

It had been folly to be pushed into buying something for which she had no real need. In California she had half a dozen negligees that had cost a couple hundred and more each, and in her suitcase at Pat's she could pick from three such expensive nighties. But all of them were used during intimate nights with other men.

She puzzled over that thought. What difference did that make?

Connie hurried back to the cocktail lounge, suddenly desperate for another drink.

Sitting, sipping an icy Martini, she tried to think back about her life as a child, when things were uncomplicated, when all a girl had to worry about was when she would get a new doll or what the folks would buy her for Christmas. Back there in the dim past were memories of being three years old and learning that another child was going to be added to the family. Later, when Pat was born, Connie had felt all the loneliness and frustration a first child experiences at the point of a second baby entering its private world. At first she both hated and loved Pat. Later, in her teens, she had always felt a strong responsibility for Pat and attempted to serve as a good example for her younger sister. Then first sex came along and a discovery that it could be fun. Too much fun!

At a party, when some of the boys spiked the punch, things got a little wild. Lights were turned out and her date started searching under her sweater. His hands felt so warm, his kisses too hot to resist. She fought him off only lightly while an inner voice screamed to let him continue—all the way! When she felt the first caress find her bra-covered breasts, all she could think of was how it might be to let him kiss her breasts.

The other couples were necking and petting hotly all around them and Connie felt suddenly cheap. Yet at the same time, wanted to know what it must be like with a boy! She heard one couple get up, leave for the back of the house. Then her date whispered, "Let's join them—in the other bed-

47

room."

She was already beyond the point of caring. The liquor buzzed in her brain, the hot driving need coursed through her. She let herself be taken in the bedroom, thinking all the time that probably nothing would really happen, yet knowing differently.

When his hands immediately slid up her legs, drew aside her skirt, pulling it up over her waist, Connie didn't want to control herself. She writhed on the bed, mentally screaming to stop him, her hands clawing at the covers, sobbing gasps of excitement trembling from her lips.

But then she felt his fingers move under the elastic band of her panties and knew it was going to be impossible to really stop him.

Then his hand was rubbing her naked flesh and she trembled up against his touch. She felt the probe of his finger enter her. After that there was no stopping him. When they started really going at one another she experienced sharp pain, but instantly a sensation of joy overwhelmed her total being. She went crazy under him.

The next day Connie felt great, longing depression. She refused to see the boy again, ever. The following month was an agony of suspense. After she had time to consider what had happened, to understand the full implications of the experience, she wondered what the mystery was all about. Her whole teenage life had been filled with fantastic wonder about sex. Now she knew from this one experience how natural a thing it was. As natural as breathing.

During this time she studied every bit of information she could get her hands on about sex and birth control. There was sadly little such information around in published form. But one pocket book was circulated among her friends called, *Love Without Fear*. Most of the kids read it for the detailed advice about sexual positions, ignoring the rest. Connie merely glanced through that section for information only and completely absorbed the rest.

"Well, hello, Connie," David's voice greeted, cutting into her reverie.

Connie jerked as if hit. Her thoughts had been so deeply alive that for a moment she felt as if he had read

48

them. As if he had been able to listen in.

"Sorry, didn't mean to startle you. What are you drinking?"

"A Martini."

"I'll order another for you, if you like." David sat down beside her, his hands falling awkwardly on the bar counter.

She studied his fine features. He had a firm chin and jaw. The slight lightening at his temples gave a sophisticated dash to his appearance. Those dark eyes, which were actually deep brown, appeared black in the dim lighting. Black and brooding—exciting. How she wanted to caress his neck, feel the texture of that black hair against her fingers. He still looked strong, broad-shouldered. She wondered if his frame was as firmly muscular as it had been eleven years before. Last night he had felt in pretty good shape. Probably not quite that hard. But years had done little to hinder his astonishing good looks.

"Nice seeing you," David said. "You caught me in the middle of a business conference. Sorry I had to be so short with you. And then...I'll admit you caught me by surprise. Yours was the last voice in the world I expected to hear on the phone."

"Why?" Connie asked, hiding the defensive reaction. "After all, I'm your sister-in-law. Nothing wrong with us having lunch together, is there?"

"Nothing, nothing in the world, I would imagine." He smiled at her, and there was a longing in his eyes, a tenderness. "You have become more beautiful, Connie."

"Years have fuzzed your mind. I'm putting on a few pounds. Have, in fact, over the years."

"Good pounds, I would say. All in the right places." He turned away abruptly, a nervous habit, Connie remembered, when he was embarrassed.

"Where's Pat?" His voice was different—detached.

"At home. I went out shopping. Wanted to be alone..." She bit her lower lip. "Well, obviously, I changed my mind at the last moment. Nothing wrong with that? Is there? Nothing wrong with a girl changing her mind, is there?"

49

"Nothing wrong," he assured her in a soft whisper.

The bartender approached then and David ordered her a Martini, a Scotch and cream for himself.

They were silent until the drinks came.

David saluted with his Scotch. "Well, good luck."

"Good luck to you."

He spotted the package on the bar at her right. "See you *did* go shopping."

There was something in his voice that sharply indicated surprise by the fact, as if he had guessed it was all a cover-up, a lie.

Was she being that transparent? She wondered.

"Of course. What'd you think? Think I'd come down to have a secret rendezvous with you?" Immediately she hated the remark. It wasn't what she had meant to imply. Or was it?

He didn't answer that. "What'd you get?"

"Oh, nothing. Just...a negligee." She hated that, too. Why had she blurted that out? A lie would have been smarter.

"Oh," was his only comment.

They were silent for a long time, finishing their drinks like two total strangers who just happened to be sitting next to each other.

When finished with his Scotch, David said:

"Want another?"

"Couldn't." She didn't dare let herself get drunk. Not with them alone like this. Not with the obvious possibility that something could happen between them if either gave a slight push.

"Hungry?"

"I guess so."

They both got up. David put two bills on the counter and then they left lounge.

"I know a good place...just outside of town." He was walking about a foot away from her; his eyes looked straight ahead, as if afraid to turn in her direction.

"Why so far? Isn't there any place around here?" She felt alarmed by his suggestion.

"It's up to you. Sure...of course. Silly of me. Just

50

down the street, *Pedro's Steak House."* Impulsively he took her arm, sweeping her along at a swift gate.

"What's the hurry?"

"Sorry, didn't realize." He dropped her arm, then took up an easier stride.

They walked in silence. She was feeling dizzy, but not from the drinks. The momentary contact of his hand on her arm had been wildly thrilling; too much so. Her pulse raced. It was difficult to think straight.

At the steak house they were met by the headwaiter, who swiftly took them to a booth in the far corner of the dining room.

"How are you, Mr. Carter?" The man eyed Connie, his face bland.

"Fine. This is Mrs. Lewis."

"The *late* Mrs. Lewis," Connie blurted out.

"My sister-in-law, visiting us," David quickly pointed out. "She's been in show business. Maybe you saw her on television."

"Is this the girl you told me about...let's see, five years ago, I would imagine. Sure, I remember seeing her on one of those TV westerns. Everybody in town was excited over it. Pleased to meet you, Miss."

Connie smiled automatically and was glad when the man left. "Sorry, I didn't mean to make that sound—I mean about the late Mrs. Lewis. I don't know what made me say that."

"Probably because you're simply glad to be finished with a...well, unhappy marriage," David offered, carefully staring at her for the first time.

"You don't know *how!"* Connie exclaimed with a light laugh. "It's not that Larry wasn't a good husband, he was all kinds of a swell guy. I just didn't love him and finally realized that a marriage without love running both ways, is a marriage not at all!"

"Why'd you do it in the first place?"

"Oh, a girl gets lonely, depressed. I don't know really, now that I think of it. He wasn't my kind of guy. Worked for an actor's agency. I had met his boss several times at 'Hollywood' parties. When I wanted a secretary job,

51

Tom offered the position. He placed me with Larry. We started dating and...well, things just fell into line—a habit formed. I was tired, like you *can't imagine!* The struggle to fight into show business can be pretty hard. You can have talent, beauty and a good knowledge of who to play along with—everything. But you have to have something more, too. Connections help, but timing has a lot to do with it. And pure luck. Maybe I never really had enough of the...what's required."

"What's that?"

"Determination. No. *More* than that! An obsession so strong that it is more important than anything else in the world. More important than breathing, than sleep, food or sex—because it becomes all of that and more. The ones who aren't lucky to make it overnight, who have to struggle for attention, because they don't have a Daddy there to push doors wide open for them, get the shit. You have to have such an impossible amount of driving hunger...to where you are blinded to everything else in the world."

"I thought that was your driving dream that...broke things up with us?" he stated rather blandly, his eyes averting from hers.

She nervously lighted a cigarette, then continued: "I had a determination to leave this town and see the big city. I wanted to be in movies, to sing with a band. I got both of them in little bits and pieces—it was enough to satisfy most of my craving desires. I tasted a little fame and wanted a little more, sure. That's only natural. But I didn't have the strength to keep it up all the time. You can take so much of a beating and your nerves, your whole being, just wants to lie down and rest, think of nothing but escaping the treadmill. You give up for a time. Some people rest for a couple of months; some wait for a couple of years, then start out again. Some continue resting. Get caught in another kind of trap— call it love, call it marriage and kids and family—or just giving up.

"It's a hard world out there! I began to think it was easier to just give up."

"Had a time of it, haven't you?"

"Yes...but don't think that's feeling sorry for myself.

52

I asked for it, Dave. What I didn't know was how difficult it would be. Damned hard."

She took a deep drag on her cigarette, blew smoke across the table toward him. "You know, they should tell that side of the story in the movie magazines. All you really hear are the stories of successful discovery. Lana Turner getting discovered at a drug store; fictions like that! Oh, they have the ones that really fought to the top; but you either don't believe it's that hard or believe you can make it up there, too. It doesn't happen that way. It's like any other kind of job, but more difficult. It is like trying to find a needle in a terrible tangled web that's so thick you can't see two feet into the endless mass. And everybody is suggesting they know the way in and through and they promise you whatever is necessary to...well...you can guess what men want. And women! Oh, let's not talk about me."

"Why not?" David inquired. "After all, I know all about myself, but so little about you, since you...left town."

She was silent for a moment, gazing at him. Then she turned away, took in the restaurant. It was one of those dimly lighted rooms where businessmen could carry on luncheon conferences with nice intimate surroundings. The dark wood panels on the walls reflected little light from the dim lanterns hanging evenly spaced from the ceiling. Southern California had plenty of such seductive dens where couples met for secret meetings, lunches that led to the nearest motel room.

For a moment Connie thought about how all this could have been hers. She might be David's wife—having lunch with him, as she would have done at least one time a month. It all seemed so natural that all at once she found it hard to believe it hadn't happened that way.

She even imagined, for a moment, that they were married, a couple, having lunch together. Then reality jarred back into place. This was very dangerous for both of them.

"Dave, I shouldn't really have come," she suddenly blurted out, looking into his eyes. "I think maybe I should go."

David grabbed her arm, as if she was about to get up and leave and he wanted to hold her back.

"Don't get silly ideas."

53

"I wasn't. Just that..." Her voice caught, and for a second it was impossible to speak. "Just that I was thinking...if I hadn't gone to Hollywood—we'd probably be married, now and having a nice innocent lunch together."

Silence slammed down on both of them. Her statement harshly underscored the implication they were dangerously close to crossing a line that shouldn't even be approached. And it started both of them.

CHAPTER FIVE

Frank Nathan's voice was harsh, biting. "Are you listening, David?"

For a moment David tried to adjust to his surroundings. How long had his mind been wandering?

"Mr. Carter!" Frank insisted, "I asked you a question."

"Sorry, Frank, just got lost...thinking about the problem." David looked up at Frank Nathan's rounded face. The man ate too much for his size and it showed. That was probably the only bad habit Frank enjoyed. His eyes were puffy, his face stiff with cold hardness, as if it had been made of stone. The heavy mouth, disapproving brown eyes seemed to criticize everything around him; especially David, at all times. There was a weakness revealed in the receding chin, accented somehow by the balding hairline. Bushy eyebrows almost met over deep-set eyes.

"What was your deep thought centering on?" Nathan demanded, nastily.

David drawing his mind away from Connie, said:

"Well, as I see it, this new line of plates should cost pennies to make—I mean in material. The art department can whip up the design—that'll run probably in man-hours-dollars something around a couple hundred hours—absorbed in the all-over cost and amounting to nothing against the total expenses. We could throw that in, as a write-off. The presses and actual material—well, with all considering, I'd say something around seven cents as a good break-even price. She's going to demand a contract giving us as little over that amount as possible. Is that the way you see it?"

Frank Nathan sat back in his swivel chair, stared

55

across the large, empty desk top at David, like some Buddha surveying its subjects with disapproval. The office around them was bare of any warmth. The few pictures that Tom Sherman, the late office manager, had hung up had been stripped off the walls and not replaced. There was a cold, business-like hardness to the room. It fitted Nathan.

"Is *that* all?" the man demanded. "We've been over that a couple of times already. I was asking you what you thought you could bring in. What can you guarantee *Barton Enterprises?* I do think we should come to some agreement on this."

David was suddenly alert. His ulcer became secondary. Nathan was talking as if he were an alien agent—not part of the company "family." It was a little trap that could close around his promotion and job. What he promised here would be *dogma!*

"I'll have to feel Freda out, see where the line can be set before making any promises. It's too soon. 1 have an appointment with her for Friday."

Those bushy black eyebrows pushed together as Nathan glared thoughtfully at him.

"I should think it would be safe ground to suggest that a twenty percent profit might be allowed. A $1,400 profit for every ten thousand. *That* would be automatic! Considering your position with the firm, I should think it would not be too much out of line to expect a fifty percent profit. You're supposed to be JB's *bright boy*—now prove it! I want to see *results!* A man wanting an assistant manager's job has to prove himself under fire. You better make a good showing, David; or I don't think JB will be very impressed. This contract can mean a lot of money in the bank for our firm. It's important, I guess you realize. Once the door is opened with Freda Hendricks, it's *all the way!* She will throw a lot of business in our direction. They will serve as one of our major clients This one contract is simply a move to open doors. Blunder on any point—we don't have a chance.

"Of course, I'll have Gordon around to back you up, if necessary. I don't want you to think of yourself as being alone on this."

David couldn't help from grinning. With Gordon

56

anywhere near this deal, the credit would be split two ways.

"I think there'll be no problem, Frank. But thanks for the offer. I know Gordon is pretty well loaded, already. But...don't worry, if I think it is necessary to call on his services, I'll do just that."

There was no question they now both understood that David had meant Gordon was supposed to keep his bloody hands off.

Frank Nathan's eyes brooded for a moment. "I don't like to tell an employee what he should do on his own time and I've always believed that a man's lunch hour is his own time. But let's be honest. An executive who drinks too much can be an ex-executive fairly quickly. Fair warning, David." Frank Nathan stood. "I know I can depend on you doing a decent job on this account!"

So concluded the meeting.

Once outside, David breathed a sigh of relief. The call to appear in Nathan's office had been waiting for him when he returned from lunch. At that moment he had not been in any mood to play any political office games with anybody. His own thoughts were too involved with the full implications of the luncheon date with Connie. He remembered the impact of her words: "*...if I hadn't gone to Hollywood—we'd probably be married now...*" and felt once more the shiver of strange, hot fear. The truth of that statement hurt. They would have been sitting there as man and wife, not brother and sister-in-law. More important was the fact that Connie had pointed this out. The rest of the lunch had been a little awkward, even creating its moments of long embarrassment. It wouldn't take much to push either of them over the line.

As David returned to his own office, he tried to focus on Pat. He picked up the phone, dialed. A moment later Pat's voice sounded over the receiver.

"Hello, honey," David greeted, hoping that the coldness of last night would have settled down by now. He had not disturbed her sleep when he got up for work.

For a brief moment silence answered him. Then her reserved voice said: "Yes, David?"

She never called him David unless she was being

57

bluntly formal.

"Honey, I was wondering...why don't we go out to dinner together. I'm sure Connie wouldn't mind being alone."

"We couldn't do that. Not on her second day here. It's out of the question! I have dinner picked out already, anyway."

"I just thought that maybe we could—"

"David, I don't know what you have in mind, but forget it!" She sounded as if she knew *exactly* what he was attempting. "After last night I don't think—"

"Pat, can't we forget last night?" He felt as if his voice was desperate sounding; but didn't care.

"Do you think *Ruth* can forget that easily?"

"Ruth has nothing to do with us."

"She certainly seemed to be important to you, last night!"

"Oh, come on, you don't really believe that."

"Why shouldn't I?" She sounded bitter. "You came right out and admitted you made a pass at her. How could you do such a thing?" Her voice caught and for a moment it seemed as if she would start crying. "I don't...want to talk about it. And I don't want to talk to you, right now."

The receiver went dead in his hands.

David sat back in his chair, hands on the desk, clasped into tight fists. Right when he needed Pat, she denied herself to him. Of course she couldn't know how serious it was. How could she guess that her own sister might suddenly create a real threat to their marriage? How could she realize that the old flame had never quite gone out and was now being fanned into a roaring fire that might consume all three of them?

He tried to turn his thoughts back to the work.

Taking a pile of correspondence from the "In" basket on his desk, David idly thumbed through it. First he separated the personal mail from business letters. When he came to a windowed envelope with *Hal's Liquor Store* printed on it, he quickly opened it.

"Dear Mr. Carter," read a note enclosed with a bill for *$367.55. "This has been past due for several weeks.*

58

Could you please remit a small payment? Thank you. Hal."

Another bill from the bank asked for a payment of *$187.50* on his car, past due. That one had slipped by accidentally.

A little later David came across a third item. Country Club dues: *$150.75.* It was due at the end of the month.

Suddenly he realized that it was impossible to pay off all these and still keep up with the normal living expenses, without cutting in too deeply in their depleting savings account.

Mentally he attempted to figure out what other outstanding *large* bills might be coming due in the next few months.

There were the summer camp charges of $50 a day for Eddie. He had wanted to send their son to a less expensive camp, but Pat had insisted on the best. *"Eddie's still so young. I have to know that he'll be taken care of by responsible people—experts. Those other places we don't know anything about. Martha said this place is the very best in the country."*

Pointing out that the others would have to be just as good, and that the fees for *Happy Hunting Grounds* were far out of line, did nothing to change Pat's determination: the *best* for Eddie. That was one point on which Pat never gave an inch.

Then there was the insurance payment that would come due the beginning of the next month for $185.76. Clothes would have to be bought for Eddie before he returned to school. That would run close to another several hundred dollars. Then he remembered with quick shock, the final payment on the Second Trust Deed on their home was due by December—*$1,750*—and property tax, which was probably going to hit a new high this year. He remembered that it had been a little over $400 last year.

David took out a piece of paper, listed the debts one by one; totaled them. Giving Eddie his first two weeks at summer camp and allowing an added hundred for property tax, at least, the total ran over $5,000; close to $6,000.

The figure staggered David. He had no idea things had gotten so far out of line. All his married life, since 1954,

59

he had managed to keep their living expenses well below his income.

Suddenly the Hendricks contract meant more than a mere promotion. It meant more money, which they could use very nicely! In fact, he either got it and a raise or he would have to start learning how to survive on potatoes until they caught up.

And this wasn't the time to cut back.

In the last three years they had managed to get themselves into a slow bind. He'd been aware of a slight growing pressure, but not known just how far it had progressed until now. At first it didn't look quite so bad. It had all been an innocent series of adding to their monthly debts. Oh, they had money in the bank, but the account had dropped from eight thousand dollars to twenty-five hundred and change—enough to cover the Second Trust Deed. The house payments were handling themselves easily enough, and they always had enough food-money on his income. The liquor supply had depleted in the last couple of months. The liquor bill had climbed far too high. They had put too much time into giving parties, which were highly expensive. He was drinking too much.

His thoughts shifted to Pat. Their sex-life had always been good. Until recently. It all tied into their spending and the almost frantic party-giving. It seemed as if both of them were approaching sex with a quiet desperation. Now that he considered it, David realized exactly how much of a change had taken place in the last year. Maybe it started with his drinking or maybe with Pat. She recently seemed overly anxious, more aggressive than he remembered from their earlier years. The first time it had startled David even if in a joyful way. But things were changing for both of them.

Problems had started one night when they were fairly high, not drunk, but a little more happy than usual—on their last wedding anniversary. When he took Pat to bed she became a tigress, aggressively seeking him out, fondling, caressing, and with such greedy need that he had lost control and in the end failed her. It didn't bother him too much then and both of them managed a good laugh about it at the time. He had given himself a double shot of Scotch. Then in the

60

darkness found Pat under the covers. The second attempt that night was highly successful and lasted far longer than most times together. But his second failure came the next week. And it wasn't funny!

David tried to count how many times in the last year he had failed Pat. Enough to shake up any man's ego. Even while sober he had fumbled. Not always, but every failure seemed to lock in more frustrating guilt, which caused more failure.

Maybe it was Pat, or a matter of their relationship dulling.

Funny, David thought. He had not considered that for several weeks. He didn't think about failure when he thought of Connie. All he knew was that she created a longing and deep desire, which overwhelmed all other ideas. It was impossible to even be near her without getting painfully aroused.

The phone ringing brought him back to the present.

"Hello, Carter speaking," he said, after picking up the receiver.

"This is Freda Hendricks. Wanted to know if you could move our appointment to tomorrow night. Something came up. I'd like to get the preliminaries over with. Do you mind?" Her voice was a mixture of brisk business and light seductiveness. It was the first personal contact he had had with Freda. But he knew her reputation. The staffs of each company had made all arrangements, up to this point.

"Let me see," David suggested, looking at his desk calendar. He already knew that tomorrow night was open but wanted to appear a little more busy and important than she might give him credit for. "Yes, I could make it—how about eight?"

"I thought for dinner. You could come over to the hotel."

It sounded like a trap for a seductive play: a maneuver for which she was famous. David didn't like it. Not at all!

"Well, my wife—"

"Oh, come on, Mr. Carter, don't tell me she doesn't like being left home, while her husband is out on a business dinner," Freda cut in sharply, before he had a chance to finish. "I know better than that. Women married to top-flight executives get used to having their husbands out on dinner appointments. I do want to settle this matter quickly. My calendar is loaded and it would be doing me a favor."

"How about eight? I don't know if I could make it any earlier. And eight is a little late for dinner."

"Mr. Carter, I do have an appointment at nine and I don't think that would give us the time we need."

"Well, unless you can make it earlier, say about four..." He felt trapped.

"It's *really* out of the question! I'll be coming back to the hotel at six-thirty—that'll give us two hours to eat and cover the ground work on our project."

She had taken over like a demon, unrelenting until he was pushed into a corner. There was nothing he could do but accept.

"Okay." Suddenly David felt foolish for having hesitated. He was probably overrating Freda Hendricks. After all, no woman could make a man do something he truly didn't want to do.

"See you then. At six-thirty? Hotel Highland, just outside of town. Room 217. Got that?"

"Okay, at six-thirty, then."

* * * * * * *

A thin, knowing smile pressed across Freda Hendricks' lovely, seductive face, as she replaced the receiver on the hook. It was going to be easier to handle this David Carter than she had hoped.

If there was one thing she knew about, it was her power over men.

Turning, she looked at the detective who was still lying naked on the hotel double bed, staring up at her.

"You still here?" Freda said with a little edge of irritation in her voice. Of course, he would be, but this was one trick to cut at a man, where it hurt the most; he'd want more action—she'd let it happen one more time with him. A quick payoff.

62

"You got what you wanted, I've only *started* with you!" The man's voice was thick as he looked at her naked body, the large breasts, which she was so proud of, the sweep and curves of her figure, kept in top form with every kind of exercise possible. Her body was part of her trade.

"Get the hell out of here! We're finished." Freda snapped. "You've had your fun—that's it!"

He leaped from the bed, suddenly had her in his iron grip, hands tightly hurting her arms. "You didn't even start!"

"I come high!"

"*Hell* you do! You're just like every other little whore. You throw those tits at a man and think that's the only thing you have to do. Well, you got yourself a *man*, here, and I'm going to get me a nice big piece of your body...I did a good job for you—you had better make it worth my while!"

Freda smiled inwardly.

It had been that way all her life. The first time she'd seen a man naked was when she was thirteen, just old enough to have sexual feelings; and she'd developed young. By accident she'd walked in on her step-father in the bathroom, and he was as startled as Freda. Nothing happened, other than embarrassment. But the sight of him naked excited her. A few months later, when dating a good looking guy who was several years older than herself, Freda had made it obvious that she wanted a little "making out"—the boy was all for it, not knowing she wanted to go all the way. When she reached down and frantically grabbed his hard, her instincts had taken over. The need had driven her into the arms of many boys, after that. It wasn't until college that Freda learned *how* to use her body.

The detective thought he was getting payment for his services, but, in actual fact, she was simply using him. Her body craved sex like a power-mad male craved money, position and devotion from any woman who might come his way. This man, like so many others in her past, was a mere toy she used for her own pleasure. She let men think they were taking advantage of her. It was a skillful game she knew exactly how to play. Controlling men was a real turn on.

63

"I like a girl who's hot. You do me a good and we'll call it even, fair enough, love!'' he demanded, gripping her head between strong hands.

Strong, thrilling hands. And driving her right into his groin.

He held her head in place while she willingly almost devoured the deliciously hardness of him. When he was almost near losing control, she pulled away. The detective was sitting on the edge of the bed and she urged him backwards, straddling his hips until she was able to surged down on the point of his shaft, letting it totally penetration her. The session didn't last long, but it was good, she had to admit that.

She paid him in full, getting far more for herself than he had gotten out of their lovemaking.

Later, when the man had left, Freda took the report he had brought and started studying it with a mounting sense of pleasure. The sucker had given it to her for a couple of orgasms and thought he'd gotten paid in full. In fact, she'd taken him to the cleaners, enjoyed the fun and games more than he might have imagined, and there would be no charges to add to her expense account. The company would be impressed at how skillfully she'd put across this deal, on the cheap, as usual, and at a swift profit for the stockholders.

David Carter would, also, come in on the cheap. Men found her kind of gamesmanship quite easy to swallow. They were all suckers for a hot, passionate woman. And they never knew she always got the best of the deal, in every way! It was always win-win for her.

* * * * * * *

Pat sat at the dinner table partly listening to the polite, but impersonal conversation spurting between David and Connie. She felt an edge of uneasiness. Why? It was hard to understand. All day the fury of anger and hurt burned at the thought of what David had done with Ruth. It wasn't that she really believed that David would ever seriously get involved with anything really out of line with Ruth! Hell, there had been plenty of chances for him to rush off into some dark corner with that woman. Both Ruth and her hus-

64

band were open about their inclination for swinging. Yet they never were a threat to anybody—being very careful and ethical. That's what was so disturbing about Ruth's emotional outburst at the party.

She looked up at Connie, still marveling over the striking perfection of her sister's beauty. Yesterday, when Connie had arrived, Pat was more or less shocked by the fact that her sister was actually more attractive than before. That was a surprise. What she had expected was hard to define. But Hollywood and some ten years struggling on her own in the big city had done great things to Connie. The woman was glamour to the hilt. A stunner. If this were not her sister it would feel terribly threatening having her stay there in their home. But she didn't consider Connie as a threat, even if knowing what had taken place years before between her and David. That was, surely, past history.

Pat realized that the years had not been so kind to herself, though. When she first met David, as a young teenage girl, she was thin, flat-chested, and frantically worried that she would never develop breasts. In the next years, maturity had given her a willowy, even attractive figure. By the time David had finished college and started dating her, she felt it possible to hold her own with other girls.

Pat had dated David because she was merely curious about him. Connie had always been the family beauty, having her choice of the most popular boys. Pat had wondered just how involved the two had been that summer. Being a few years younger and far more innocent than Connie, Pat spent many nights speculating on her sister's long dates with David. Connie never talked much about them and the mystery deepened. So when David suddenly asked her out, the idea seemed fascinating. Later she found herself falling in love with him. When he proposed, she suddenly feared that it might not be merely for love of her, but because of some vague remembrance of Connie. By then she guessed what might have taken place that one summer between him and her sister. Smart as David had been in college, finishing it a year sooner than other young men, Pat had realized that he knew little or nothing about his own emotions. Pat had come to believe herself foolish for having thought he was still in

65

love with Connie. Pat was honest concerning her feelings about David and her sister. She wasn't jealous. Connie was out in Hollywood. Years split her from David and it was hardly logical that she could really still mean anything to him. Yet when he proposed, Pat wanted to be completely sure of him before wedding bells united them in marriage. So she put off the wedding for six months.

That first night, after their engagement, when David had suggested they go up to his apartment for dinner, Pat only hesitated a moment, then accepted, knowing exactly what would happen. She was a little frightened; partly for the same reason any girl is hesitant to give her virginity up before marriage, but also because this would be the final test. Or so she thought of it. Would David be comparing her with Connie? It was then that Pat admitted to herself that he surely must have had an affair with her sister. It was certainly logical enough.

She had prepared dinner, while David fixed cocktails and arranged the dining area with candles and soft background music. Pat remembered little of the dinner itself because all her thoughts were centered on what would happen afterwards. Since they were engaged she felt no guilt about letting David make love to her. Also, somewhere along the line, she had heard that it was best to find how well mated you were with the man about to become your husband, before marriage locked your lives together. Sex was not everything, Pat knew now, and had guessed then, but it was very important. If sex fizzled out between a man and woman, the rest was sure to crumble. Sex was part of the foundation of marriage and if the foundation began to weaken, the house would start to show signs of breaking down. Maybe Connie had told her that. She couldn't remember.

Later they had danced a little in his small living room, then when David kissed her, she knew that the real thing was starting. That kiss drove both of them toward the bedroom. They laughed a lot, teased each other about being naked, then made love.

She remembered the first thrill of his hands on her naked breasts as if it had happened yesterday. She reached for him. But beyond that, everything was a blur; she only

66

remember the thrilling sensations of being in his arms, feeling his kisses, caresses. And later hardly felt the first pain as he made her a real woman; she merely felt smothered with the realization that he had become a part of her; so intimate and loving a part that it made her want to cry.

She had wanted to plead to have him "fuck" her all night, never stop. She never used such words, but knew them. Sometimes she wanted to say them to Dave, but didn't. In recent years the temptation had become stronger to be more open, more aggressive, brazen, even shocking. But she had read somewhere that some men expected their wives to be a Virgin Goddess. But even friends of hers claimed to talk that way during sex.

And not just swingers like Ruth.

Maybe that was what had terrified her the other night. Ruth would just love to ball it with David; and Pat wasn't quite sure about her husband; not any more. It wasn't that she didn't trust him; or believe he might be losing interest in her; simply that he was at that stage in life when a man might begin to doubt his sexual abilities. His failures during the last year were obviously bothering him. And that might drive him into the arms of another woman.

The thought terrified Pat.

How could a happily married couple ever entertain the idea of seeking outside lovers? She didn't understand Ben and Ruth.

Pat had never been even interested in another man.

Pat turned her thoughts back to the present with painful effort. She felt hard, frantic fear that David was dangerously at the point of seeking extra-marital sex. It wasn't even rational for he had never really shown signs of a roving eye. Not until the other night with Ruth.

What had changed things? What was different? Only the event of Connie's visit suggested a possible explanation.

Suddenly she was looking at her sister, and a strange sense of jealousy raged up. It wasn't right that any woman could still look that good at her age. Pat knew that, unlike her sister, she was already showing signs of aging. Little wrinkles had settled around her eyes and mouth, the texture of her neck seemed less smooth. When she looked at herself

67

in the mirror, signs of years of marriage and childbirth marked her stomach and breasts ever so slightly. She had begun to notice, consciously, that she wasn't a kid any more.

Pat looked at David.

He was gazing at Connie, unaware that anybody noticed. There was an odd, pensive expression in his eyes as they ran over Connie's face.

Pat suddenly felt lost. *What was he thinking?*

"Oh, David, would you like some more potatoes?" she blurted out much too loudly.

Both Connie and David turned.

"No—no!" David shook his head. "Wonderful roast, dear. I couldn't eat another thing."

"You hardly touched your food," Pat accused, studying his plate. The peas and potatoes were only half eaten.

"Sorry, honey. Wasn't too hungry." He looked guilty, Pat decided.

She fought down a sense of frustration. *What's getting into me?*

She thought of Eddie, off at summer camp and was vaguely glad that he wasn't home right now. Immediately she wondered why that should be important. Automatically she looked at Connie, then David.

Alarmed, Pat saw all at once exactly why she was frightened. It wasn't what David had done the night before with Ruth, but the fact that Connie was staying with them. David was ripe for an affair with another woman. Pat knew that his occasional failures at sexual intercourse were bothering him more than he even realized. Probably much the same way her own doubts about the loss of youth plagued her. Now, with Connie in the mix, Pat knew she had never been quite sure if David had completely gotten over her sister. That part of his life had always been shaded in mystery: underdeveloped in its explanations. The fact that David had never really been willing to talk much about Connie, in any manner, suddenly became obvious to Pat.

"How about drinks?" Pat offered, feeling the need of a stiff shot.

"Sure," David quickly agreed; too quickly! "I'll go fix them. Scotch all around?"

68

"Don't you have gin?" Connie inquired.

"Sure, mix a swell Dry Martini."

David left the room and suddenly Pat felt horribly alone. She looked at Connie and knew that this woman, her own sister, might be a real threat to her marriage.

That was a stunning shock. A surprise. And it shouldn't have been. It was so obvious. Such a totally stunning woman who had been David's early love. How important had that summer been to either of them, to both of them?

And what did she really know about her sister? Eleven years was a long time. They had been almost totally out of contact during that period. They really didn't know one another any more. Before they had been children. Now they were fully mature women with a past filled with experiences totally alien to one another.

If Connie weren't her sister the threat would have been obvious right from the start. Now Pat was beginning to piece together a whole series of clues, dangers, imagined or real.

Connie was like a stranger; a woman on the make; a woman who might want David. And was there anything stopping her from taking what she wanted? What kind of Hollywood experiences had molded her adult morality? That town had certainly offered its perversions and its twisted sense of right and wrong, with pawing bodies reaching out in the night to any beautiful creature within reach. Suddenly Pat was imagining all kinds of grotesque images, nightmarish fantasies created out of endless magazine stories about Tinsel Town.

A cold shiver coursed down Pat's spine as she fought the raging jealousy, the hard suggestion of hate and terrible fear.

Was her sister the kind of Hollywood tramp that took men to bed just for kicks?

Connie had always been somewhat wild. And her years in California could hardly have dulled that wildness. In fact it must have sharpened it into some kind of mad obsession that feasted on human flesh like some demon monster from another universe.

Pat laughed at her thoughts. Now she was really having mad fantasy illusions.

"What's so funny?" Connie wanted to know.

"Oh, well, nothing. Just wondering how much Hollywood changed you."

"Oh. You'd be surprise," her sister said, eyes scanning the room as if trying to find a place to focus on.

"Is it as...wild as they say in the magazines?" Pat inquired. She had never really asked Connie much about that. Here was a person who had actually experienced that world.

"Oh, wild enough."

"In what way?"

"Every way. Not anything like here...."

"Yes. You always called this Small Town, U.S.A."

"You remember that!" Connie smiled, now her eyes connected with Pat's. "Sometimes...I longed for the closeness. It can get terribly lonely—and it is hard out there. Show-biz isn't all fun and games, believe me."

"I suppose not," but Pat had no real understanding about all that. Her life had always been centered on family, Dave, her son, this town.

"You never really understood much about me, did you?" Connie observed, thoughtfully. "No. Don't defend that. I meant, we're so different. I wanted out. Desperately wanted that—and, well, I suppose that's what I got."

"You sound...bitter."

"No. Just...well, I'm realistic."

"What was it like out there in Sunny Southern California?"

"Oh, sunny I guess.... I'll have to tell you all about it one of these days, if you really want to know."

"Oh, I do. Really do," Pat announced, suddenly feeling closer to Connie. For some reason it seemed as if this short conversation had bridged some of the distance between them.

Yet, Connie was still a stranger. And a wonderfully vibrant woman beautifully packaged with sophistication.

Was she really a threat?

Pat, again, felt all the doubts rush into her.

At that point David returned, bright and a bit too cheerful as he handed the drinks all around.

70

His eyes seemed to rush over Connie, lingeringly, the sweep away, almost guiltily.

Was that illusion or real?

"Well, ladies, bottoms up!"

That sounded frighteningly risqué in Pat's mind. Suddenly she had this instant mental picture that was quite scary.

Could she possibly compete with Connie for David's affections?

Suddenly Pat felt very uneasy, very frightened, uncertain. She gulped on the drink, not looking at either her sister or husband.

"Well, ladies, what were you all talking about?"

"Oh, nothing much," Connie offered.

"I was asking about her experiences in Hollywood," Pat quickly offered, nervously reaching for a cigarette.

"And I was saying some other time," Connie quickly offered.

"Well, we have a famous actress in our home!" David announced a little too loud.

"Hardly, Dave. Just a struggling one who never made it really at all."

"You make that sound terribly sad."

"Well it isn't a great success story. They're quite human out there...just like here. People are people. Only it is very tough getting into that game. A closed shop. And you have to really work your ass off. I'd rather talk about anything other than that."

Pat's mind iced over. The fear was shuttering all rational thought. She tried, desperately, to be pleasant, warm. But sounded a bit nervous in her own mind. Every time she looked at Connie or David she continued to look for signs that would reinforce her fears. She wanted to scream at the very walls. But instead tried to appear casual and social. Yet nothing made much impression on her, other than the continually grown alarm, suspicion that something was surely going on between Connie and David. She finished her drink and then was suddenly aware that it had been somehow refilled. Also they had moved into the playroom. The conversation was a blur that made little impression on her mind.

Maybe it was full of silences. She ran with it, nodding, smiling and commenting without focused thought. Party games: social retorts on automatic. Every thought was tortured by the sudden realization that Connie's visit might turn into a marital divide—and she felt helpless to advert it from happening.

If it happened, would things ever be the same? Of course they wouldn't!

CHAPTER SIX

David noticed that the drinks seemed to have made Pat a little more warm and friendly. The evening "cool" she had worn was melting slightly. For that he was glad. All during dinner there had been a mild stiffness, but not only on Pat's side. Just simply that her uncommunicative attitude had done little to help Connie or himself.

Now they were sitting in the playroom, drinks served all around, the fireplace crackling with flames. Pat was on the sofa next to him, Connie to their left, in the large pink lounge chair; legs propped up on the low footstool. She kept her gaze centered on the fire, looking up only when a remark was directed her way.

David had not placed his arm around Pat. It never paid to push his wife too quickly out of one of her moods. She would allow the freeze to melt at its own short rate.

They were on their second drink. Only the fireplace brightened the room. David found it hard to keep his eyes from moving to Connie especially since she was almost in his line of vision. The fire played colorfully on the sheer nylon stockings. The thrust of her breasts seemed accented by a thin line of flickering light. She looked seductive and cuddly. Hellishly seductive.

Pat suddenly said: "You should see the darling nightie Connie got today."

Connie shot a glance toward her sister, then looked at David. "It's nothing, really."

"Oh, it's really cute." Then in a nervous, hurried voice, "You should see her in it! Not *really!* I mean—"

"Never fear—" Connie said too lightly. "Such things are not for married men to gaze upon."

73

Awkwardness set in the atmosphere. Pat replied: "Of course. I don't know what made me say that. I didn't mean it the way it sounded."

"Hey," David laughed, tensely, "what's with you two?"

Neither of them answered; so he continued with: "I should take the both of you out on the town."

Pat started to say something, but Connie beat her to it. "I'm exhausted. Honestly. But it's been nice. Maybe I'll turn in early." She pressed her lips together, then nodded as if to herself. "Yes, come to think of it, I *should* be tired. All that partying last night—didn't get to bed until very late."

"And then not in your own bed. Meant to thank you about that," David quickly put in. Then he explained to Pat. "She found me pretty plastered. The dear put me in her bed—"

"Oh?" Pat sounded alarmed. She was like rigid stone on the sofa.

Connie laughed. "I slept out here, silly. He was too...well; I really couldn't let him sleep here. After all, this is his home and—well, you two weren't on speaking terms and—"

"Pat...it...well, I was all upset about you and—"

Pat turned to him, her face soft with wifely love. Tiny wrinkles formed around her eyes, her lips parted, dimpling. "Dave, I'm so sorry about all that. It was ridiculous of me to...get all worked up...well, I'll make it up to you."

Connie laughed. "I guess *that's* a cue for me to do a disappearing act."

Pat flashed her a startled look. "I didn't mean it *that* way."

"Look, sis, don't start apologizing to me. If I guess right, the two of you are a healthy, happy married couple. Maybe its time to say good-night and let you work out your own problems, alone. There is a time and a place for outsiders and—"

"You're no outsider, Connie," Pat quickly put in.

"Of course not, Connie," David managed, suddenly feeling things had gone too far out of line. The conversation was thick with innuendo, weighted down with awkward po-

74

liteness and something else he could not quite label. Nonetheless they were acting like players speaking the poorly written dialogue of a hack writer.

Connie stood, stretched and yawned. It was an unfortunate act, for her breasts surged out against the pink sweater, her body took on a lustful wild animal stance, creating a quick reaction within him. She glided to the door like a graceful doe; "I'm tired and going to bed. I hope you don't mind."

David thought she seemed to put a slight perverse tone to the word bed; but figured he merely imagined it.

Then she disappeared down the hall. They heard the guestroom door open and close.

For some time both sat in silence—neither moving.

"How was work today?" Pat inquired, opening the conversation. She stared at the empty glass in her hands, held on her lap.

"Oh...nothing special, other than the fact that I was sorta forced into a dinner-date tomorrow night. The Hendricks deal."

"Important, isn't it?"

"Important enough to change our lives. If I pull this off there should be a promotion."

"We could use the extra money," Pat said simply. Then: "I need a drink. How about you?"

David considered. He looked up at his wife as she stood over him, slim, delicate, and so feminine. The fire played highlights over her body. She was quite different from Connie—and just as attractive in her own way. A more delicate maturity.

"Mad at me, still?"

She smiled crookedly, shook her head, and the short hair swished slightly from side to side. "No, I'm not mad. Not any more, Dave."

"Then maybe I shouldn't have another drink?"

Her eyes flashed. "Are you making naughty suggestions?"

"Why not? You *are* my wife, aren't you?"

"Don't you know for sure?" she teased, moistening her lips with the tip of a delicate tongue.

75

He stood, pulled her intimately close. "I guess I do."

He touched her lips with his own, tenderly; they parted wide to the kiss and he allowed his tongue to play gently along her teeth, and then probe deeper. Her body tensed and he felt a caressing hand touch the back of his neck as he squeezed her fanny.

"I do want a drink, Dave," she moaned as they broke the embrace.

"Want me to get it for you?"

"That would be nice. I could...get into something else. Would you like that?" She was trying too hard to please him.

"I would like that."

As she turned he playfully tapped her fanny.

"Naughty boy." Pat half ran out of the room.

David stood there thinking about Pat. She would probably put on her white negligee, a filmy gown he had picked out some years before, because of its transparency. She looked lovely in it.

Then he thought about the negligee Connie had bought and wondered what it was like. Probably very bold in its sexual visibility.

A tingle teased David. He suddenly realized he had a painful erection.

Connie was in the room down the hall, far away from the master bedroom.

David decided that he very much needed a drink after all and went into the den. He poured a shot into a glass and quickly downed it. The liquor burned at his stomach, then sent soothing fingers over his nervous system.

Slowly he prepared a Scotch and soda for Pat, then started across the playroom. As he came to the hall, he looked to the left, towards the guestroom. How easy it might be to walk in on Connie. She would let him have her; he was convinced of that.

Pat was waiting for him.

David turned, walked toward the bedroom.

"Okay if I come in?" he inquired at the door, feeling formal in his guilt.

"*Never,* you evil man!" Pat's bubbling laughter

sounded through the wooden panel.

The door opened and Pat stood there, the white negligee like loose fog around her slender, nicely developed body. He could see the sharp points of her breasts press against the cloth, the rounded angle of her hips, the naked thighs and legs.

Quick needles of excitement attacked David, as his body reacted hotly to the sight of his wife.

He kissed her lightly, stepped into the room and kicked the door shut.

She glided across the room to the large king size bed, with its lacy pink spread doubled back. The covers were in place, pillows arranged above the striped sheets. The dim light on the dresser had been turned on, and soft music played from the clock-radio.

Pat looked so girlish and attractive in her eagerness for him. "How about that drink, Dave?"

He sat on the bed and she took the drink. Her hands seemed to tremble slightly.

Touching his thigh, Pat said: "Why don't you get more comfortable. You would look silly trying to make love to me in that outfit."

Her lips smiled knowingly, in open, easy invitation.

"Come on," she encouraged, lying back against the bed backboard. "You don't want to keep me waiting all night. It's been almost two weeks since we made love."

"So long?" He stood, moved to the adjoining bathroom. "I didn't realize."

"You *are* a dear. You get so involved with your work...I would imagine that time sort of gets all jumbled up." She was being very wifely, very understanding and maybe a little too eager. It was almost as if Pat had turned into a different woman.

David started getting undressed.

Pat laughed, teasing him with her eyes. *"Why* you naughty boy. You're a rock!"

David felt immediate embarrassment.

"Oh, darling, don't be silly," Pat told him, reading the expression on his face correctly. She motioned him into bed. "Come here, darling—I do love you so."

Laughing, Pat urged him down to her. Their bodies immediately took on a well-practiced position, giving play to the more intimate centers, teasing one another with fingers, hands, creating the quick urge, the surging tender pleasure that would lead to wild passion.

Both of them were caressing and searching one another, kissing, hugging, tenderly, then more passionately stroking the deepest centers of their beings, both physically and emotionally. It was like riding a wave that just rolled over him, like a wonderful drunk.

Then Pat seemed to sense his need and her hands reached around, caressed his back, urging him down until their lips met, open, moist, tongues voluptuously drinking upon one another, making him heady with hot fire.

Her hips surged up and he felt the warmth and moisture of her against him. They both responded to the intimate contact.

Suddenly, like two practiced lovers used to one another through wonderful years of intimacy, they rolled and Pat was on top of him and as if reading his thoughts, she lifted as he frantically thrust, missing, desperate and wild. She tried to help him. In a frenzied move, David again attempted to enter Pat.

His mind screamed *I can't fail her! I can't, now!*

Then he felt the wonderful soft moisture surrounding him as he thrust in deep, experienced and sudden voluptuous pleasure. A combination of love and passion, tenderness and greed folded around him like a violent vice and became *too* much! He froze, afraid to even breathe; afraid to think knowing the control was slipping away. One spark and it would be over.

Pat moved and he half sobbed as he felt the bursting discharge ripple up from deeply within him, flooding a climactic end to what became the beginning. What might have been pleasure was smothered by the frustration and guilt of failing Pat. All that was left was sexual release without the erotic ecstasy.

Some vague awareness of being alone, of Pat's body fading away out of existence, impressed itself on David. It could have been a moment. It might have been several minutes. He felt sick. Pat was still lying there, her body tensed, hands clawed into the covers, face lined with anguished pain. She didn't say anything as he moved from the bed. David knew he should orally satisfy her but didn't have the strength. All he wanted to do was find a deep grave to bury himself in—away from the shame. He didn't have the ability to do anything other than feel sick.

He had failed; bitterly failed. *Oh God, how he had wanted to do it good, to set up an example to himself and Pat; to prove that everything was normal and right between them*

David went into the bathroom, his stomach suddenly on the verge of heaving. He made it just in time. Once the convulsive jerking had settled down, David leaned against the door, fighting the guilt, forcing himself to admit that it wasn't his fault, that he couldn't help it. The drinks and Pat's body had merely been too strong a combination to take all at once; he tried to tell himself.

But it didn't help.

* * * * * * *

Pat's body slowly relaxed, felt the need simmer out, the frustration gradually lessen.

She felt both irritation at David's failure and a great pain of sympathy, knowing that it was far more painful for him.

What hurt Pat most was her own realization of how important a successful union had been. A man never stepped out on a wife who could keep him happy in bed. If he failed, for *any* reason, the danger of having to share him with another woman became more probable.

She felt helpless, because it had not been her fault and there was nothing she could really do to help him. This was something he would have to face alone. She would merely be able to stand by him; be there when he needed her understanding and love.

As David returned from the bathroom, started for the—door, Pat moved, called out. "David, please. Come here."

79

"No...I want to think."

"Please, Dave. Don't make so much of it. It wasn't your fault. Please, come to me." She sat up, looked at him, pleading with her eyes.

He hesitated, his right hand on the doorknob. Slowly he started to release the doorknob and then faced her and moved forward. He came into her arms, a half sob bursting from deep within his throat.

"Pat, I'm sorry..." he said.

"Don't, Dave, please, don't. It's all right. It wasn't your fault. I love you..." she countered over his words, caressing the back of his head. "I love you, Dave. That's all that matters. Please, don't hurt yourself like this. It's not worth it."

Suddenly he stopped speaking, then slipped down onto the bed next to her. He pulled her close.

"You're wonderful, Pat. Wonderful. I don't know how I deserve a wife like you. Most women would hate a man for—"

"No, they wouldn't!" Pat told him firmly. "All women, at one time or another, face the same kind of problem. You aren't any different than most men, in that way. I'm no different than all their wives who love them. If you were sleeping out—that would he different." She bit her lower lip for having said that. "I mean. Dave, after all, we love each other—this will pass. You are a wonderful lover; you know that. So you screw up...or don't screw up...once in a while." She laughed at that, startled by this attempt to make a joke. But it all sounded forced. "Nobody can be perfect, all the time."

"Let's not talk." He touched her stomach.

His hand reached up and touched her breasts and Pat felt a sharp stab of need and pleasure as his palm pressed gently against the tight nipple.

She reached up, pulled his caress away.

"Don't, David. Not again. tonight."

"Please, honey," he said, desperate. "Trust me."

His free hand caressed across her hips and she tensed under the touch. A wild erotic wave of need attacked her nerves as he caressed again with more forceful intent. She

80

sighed, sick, because it was now impossible to stop him. He would caress and caress and kiss and kiss her until hot release gave rest to the burning nerves. But she wanted the full course, not just the snack. She wanted to feel the surge of him unite completely to her body.

But when his lips rapidly caressed down across her belly and then swiftly lower, she sobbed, arched up against his kisses, hands suddenly gripping the back of his head, greedily encouraging him.

Pat trembled, writhed, thrashing about on the bed, her head jerking from side to side against the pillow. Her throat constricted, her voice murmured words, moans, crying for him to continue, sobbing breathless commands as the mounting pleasure burst into a convulsive throb.

She was clawing at the bed. Now frantic with desire. Wanting him to enter her, to feel the fullness of him, deep inside.

Suddenly she felt his lips lift away, then she jerked as if struck by electric fire as his finger penetrated her.

She sobbed, every nerve curling up; each muscle sensually tensed against the sudden pleasure deep caressing.

God! Her mind screamed. *If only it was the real thing.*

Then all awareness bubbled away and another climax attacked her. Slowly the knowledge that she was alone came into focus; then exhaustion ebbed consciousness out of existence.

* * * * * * *

David had finished the drink and was sitting at the den bar still lost in his thoughts about Pat and Connie and himself. He felt better now that it had been possible to relieve his wife to some degree. At least he hadn't failed in his husbandly duty. Afterwards she had fallen into a deep restful sleep. After lying beside her for some time unable to relax, he had come here for a drink.

He poured another Scotch, added cream, then sipped from the glass.

Suddenly he wondered if it were Pat's fault. She had

81

changed. His own failures had started after that change. But he couldn't blame Pat; her more bold sexual acts were quite exciting, not the reverse.

Then maybe *he* had changed. Would he fail with Connie? The thought scared David. He was shocked that it was possible to sit there so calmly and even consider Connie.

Automatically his eyes went in the direction of Connie's room. He wished she would get out of his life; go back to Hollywood or anyplace—back to where she *belonged!*

Bitter resentment knifed him. The timing was off. Or would it have been the same, no matter what? They couldn't forever ignore one another.

He left the den, not actually aware of doing so.

Upon stopping in front of the closed guestroom door, David snapped out of the daze, numbed by the very fact he stood there.

His body surged with frustrated need, hands shook, damp with sweat.

A mental vision of Connie lying nude in bed, the covers tucked in around her youthful, ripe form waiting for him to slip in beside her, crazed his mind.

David swallowed hard, gut tightened. He felt erotic waves float over him and realized that his body was fully heated, needing. Then as he became aware that his right hand was on the doorknob, he released it as if made of red hot metal.

Minutes later he was in bed, next to his wife, aware of her even breathing.

He faced her in the darkness, tried to make out the form of her features, but only saw a mental picture of Connie.

Frantic, David reached out, touched Pat's shoulder and then kissed the soft velvet of her neck.

Pat murmured, then turned away.

His hand reached out and found her hip, naked, soft and warm.

For an instant he was tempted to awaken her; relieve the hard need that burned like fire through him.

But this erected throb was for Connie! All it wanted was to feel her wrapped around it.

82

Instead, he lay back, tried counting backwards in an attempt to relax the tight hurting pressure. How long it was before sleep came, David didn't know. And even then, reality faded into a perverted dream-fantasy that made it difficult to tell where one had ended and the other started:

> Connie's naked body was lying on the bed, her legs spread wide, her lush lips taunting him voluptuously. "Come on love, you got a thing there that can really do me right!"
>
> David realized he was naked, too, just feet away from Connie.
>
> Then another voice chanted hauntingly from his left.
>
> He turned to see Ruth.
>
> "You taunted me the other night, but now...you won't get away from me!"
>
> Her hands were suddenly on him, her naked breasts almost touching his chest. Her voice was lusty as she said: "You have a big, lovely and I want to really have it gift wrapped in me!"
>
> Connie's voice taunted him from the bed, saying: "Come to me, dear, remember you're mine. You'll always be mine. And you know it!"

Suddenly David felt the dream splatter away and realized that the sun was brightly shining across his face. He was sweating, the dream all too vivid in his mind.

Pat's voice came in sweetly from the distance, saying: "Time to get up, honey. You told me to, wake you early."

CHAPTER SEVEN

The desk clerk looked up as David approached. "What can I do for you, sir?"

"My name's Mr. Carter, I'm supposed to meet a Freda Hendricks. Room 217, I believe."

His eyes wandered around the lobby of the Highland Hotel. The walls were heavy looking, with dark-wormwood. Huge chandeliers hung from the high ceiling. There were several tropical plants placed around the lobby. On the walls were about a dozen paintings, mostly done in oil, rich in color, realistic in style.

The desk clerk said: "Yes, there's a message here for you."

David took the envelope the man handed him, tore it open, read the quickly scrawled note:

> *Be a little late, please make yourself at home. Have a couple of drinks on my tab. Best. Freda.*

"Thank you," David said to the clerk. "Could you tell me where the cocktail lounge is?"

"Over there, to the right."

David felt foolish, because a small, gold painted sign over an open doorway announced *Cocktail Lounge* not ten feet away. Only a blind person could miss it.

As he stepped into the dim confines of the lounge, he felt suddenly alone, slightly ill at ease. The place was all but empty. One couple was hidden away in a corner booth and appeared as if they were having some illicit romantic meeting. David quickly pushed that thought out of his mind.

84

Probably just a married couple.

Stepping up to the oak bar, he sat on one of the red leather stools. After ordering a Scotch, David surveyed his surroundings with one quick sweep of his eyes.

It was a quiet, intimate, but conservative place, with a mirrored wall behind the bar, fronted by scores of bottles. Booths were lining the opposite wall and small cocktail tables filled in the space between.

When the drink came, he gulped it down nervously. His mind whispered the last parting statement Harvey Peterson had made in his office a half-hour before.

The man had come into the office about five-thirty and started talking about Connie.

"She's something great!" he announced. "And I thought we were headed right for home plate. It was hard to read her. I heard you dated her years ago. Is that true?"

"Sure, sure." He was annoyed by the whole conversation and wanted to drop it. Almost brutally he said: "But right now I have other problems, to be quite frank! This new account."

"Yeah, I'd love your problems, buddy. That's some lady you'll be seeing from what I've heard. You married guys get all the breaks."

"It's business."

"Of course. And her kind, so I've been told, is to fry her deals with a lot of sex tossed in for a closer. I've seen her in action at a convention last year. She was hanging all over some guy and her body was pasted into such a revealing dress. Rumors were flying. And she closed the deal and the man looked totally...well, she apparently wiped him out in a very generous manner!"

"Oh, for God's sake knock it off, Harv!"

Then the last parting exchange. "Well, don't say I didn't warn you, David. I've seen her in action. She's a powerhouse! I've heard she'll screw you one way or the other—at the drop of a hat. Man, are you the lucky one! Why don't I get shots like that?"

That line kept racing through David's brain as he sat in the cocktail lounge waiting for the woman in question.

David ordered another Scotch, sure that the liquor

would hardly affect him enough to be noticed. Normally he believed in remaining stone sober during work. He was half way through the Scotch, when his name was called out.

"Yes?" David said to the bellboy in the red uniform who was standing not five feet away.

"There's a message for you. The desk clerk can tell you."

David paid for the two Scotches, finished off what was left in his glass and followed the young man out into the lobby.

The clerk said: "Miss Hendricks just called from her room. Asked for you to go on up."

David tensed inwardly and felt another stab of ulcer pain. He was acting like a school kid! Freda Hendricks couldn't be a man-eater, so there was nothing to get alarmed about. No woman could make a man do anything against his will and he wasn't about to allow himself the mistake of being seduced by the woman, no matter what.

He made his way up to the second floor, then found room 217. Hesitating only long enough to balance his briefcase under his left arm, David knocked on the door.

Almost immediately it opened.

The first stunning blow hit him then because, with all the warning and expectation, he had not really known what to expect. A female lawyer with the reputation of being a hard businesswoman, didn't add up to what stood before him.

Long red hair flowed over her shoulders in straight lines. Her face was strikingly beautiful, soft and feminine, the nose slightly turned up, the eyes, bright green and large, almost innocent. She had a sensual, full mouth, lined deep red. The odor of exotic perfume assailed his nostrils like an overwhelming erotic stimulant. Her body was packed into a green shoulder less dress, which heaved the large mounds of her breasts up and out, revealing a sharp depth between.

"Come on in," Freda invited in a low, haunting voice. It was an intimate invitation spiced with challenge. Her eyes flashed over his body as if feasting on every inch. "I'm sorry to have kept you waiting, but I came in a few minutes late and wanted to change into something more presentable. I

86

hope you'll find the accommodations to your liking."

Her voice was business-like, but the visual packaging was down right seductive.

She glided back and waited until he had passed her, then closed the door.

The sound of the latch moving into place was almost like the loud slamming of a padlocked door of some strangely perverse jail from which nobody could escape without the master key, which the mistress of the house kept, locked up in the depths of her body.

He felt trapped.

The room had a high ceiling with large wooden beams crossing it lengthwise. The opposite wall was made of glass, giving an excellent view of the city beyond, upon which the sun was brightly setting in a flash of red-oranges.

"It looks a lot better at night, with the sparkling lights of town like little jewels against black velvet," Freda Hendricks explained. "By the way, I've ordered dinner up here. I hope you don't mind. It'll be easier to carry on our business in that fashion."

Her head nodded to the table, which was placed in front of the window with two chairs on either side. A white tablecloth had been spread out with shiny silverware and white china. Two candles centered the small table. A bucket of ice with a bottle of champagne was placed to one side, on a tiny stand.

He started to say something, but she interrupted before he had even opened his mouth.

"I'll admit, 1 really don't like eating out—I mean, in restaurants. One does get tired of such things, you know. The quiet and peace of a more intimate dinner in this kind of setting appeals to me. Having the chef fix up two special steaks, my recipe of wine sauce. Stuffed potatoes and green baby peas. They'll be up in about thirty minutes, gives us some time to get acquainted, drink a little champagne and check each other out. Always like to feel the opposition out a little before getting down to the hard cut of business. Don't you agree?"

She had taken over completely, with a skill that was frightening. And while her words were politely correct and

87

tone of voice evenly shaded, there was just a hint of subtle seduction to the way they were arranged, as if she'd calculated them to imply much more without being too obvious.

David merely nodded, trying to ignore the large double bed to his right. All they needed was the intimate darkness of night and background music to make the setting a total sexual trap. But the woman wasn't being quite that obvious. She knew the game and it was her show, her stage and her script.

"Would you pour the champagne?" she requested, sitting down on the bed.

Oh, that was cute, he realized. Let him appear to be in some kind of control, by doing the champagne thing.

"No place to park ourselves...except the chairs and *here.*" She smiled, warmly, not quite a sexual invitation. "I was wondering what you would be like, David. You don't mind my calling you David, do you? You simply must call me Freda. Might as well get on first name terms right from the beginning. Saves a lot of embarrassment and awkwardness later, don't you think?"

David nodded, went to the champagne. In moments he had the bottle open and was pouring their drinks.

"You did that very well," Freda announced, coming to his side. "Most men make a big pop out of it and foam spurting all over the place. I like a man who is neat and orderly. How'd you do it?"

"Just a case of twisting, rather than pushing with the thumbs." David raised his glass as she took hers.

"Well," she saluted, tapping his glass, "to a successful and pleasant relationship."

"I'll drink to that much," Dave countered, wanting to close his eyes on the vision of her sensual beauty.

It was the old game, but with a new twist.

Usually an out-of-town executive would be presented with a female escort, who was highly paid for her services. Once he had been wined and dined and then later screwed royally all night, it was far easier to get his full cooperation the next day. He would happily make deals with the company who had hired the woman. The implied promise was more of the same kind of royal consideration throughout the

88

relationship.

Here, Freda served as the full course, all wrapped up into one stunning package. A highly more effective manner of doing business. No wonder she was so successful.

She tossed her head prettily to one side, the flaming red hair shifting back and forth on her shoulders. "You aren't what I expected."

"Oh?"

"No. I thought maybe you might be a more...well ... older man. You're...well different, to say the least. You'd be surprised how many executives are a little on the senior side. You look like a young healthy animal to me." She laughed lightly at that last. "Maybe thirty-three, thirty-five at the most." She was taking in his body as if it were some delectable goodie that she found very interesting. "Am I what you expected?"

"No, not really." David took a sip of his champagne, turned, looked for some place to sit and found only the bed, other than the two chairs at the table, which were, apparently, being saved for dinner.

"Maybe," he suggested quickly, turning back to her, "we should run over a bit of the groundwork before dinner."

She reached out, her long tapered fingers touched his arm, almost caressing, but not quite; restraining him. "No, not right now. After dinner we can worry about such things. I'd rather get to know something about you."

"What do you want to know?"

"Are you married? But of course, you mentioned your wife to me yesterday. Is she attractive? I'll answer that. She's attractive or you wouldn't have married her."

"What makes you say that?" He sounded defensive.

"A good-looker like you would get a good looking wife. Simple addition." She raised a neatly marked eyebrow, smiled as if pleased with herself. "See, doesn't take a detective to figure that one out. Bet you have a boy."

"Yes, seven years old. Off to summer camp, right now."

"Your wife misses him, I would guess. I would think she is a real homebody." There was just the edge of tiredness to her voice as she spoke, suggesting the idea was a bit bor-

89

ing.

"She loves Eddie, if that's what you mean. But then, she's hardly the homebody." Again he sounded defensive. "What makes you say that?"

"Oh, most girls who live in towns like this are homebodies. The ones who aren't, don't stay. They move on to more exciting places, to enjoy a more exciting life. Some seek careers, like mine. Some...well, get married to rich men. Or...there are endless variables. See what I mean? Simple addition." She moved to the bed, and her rounded hips made sensual rolling movements. She moved like an animal in heat. But in such a natural way that it didn't come across as an obvious seductive come on.

"You know, David," Freda said softly, as she sat down on the end of the bed, "I came from such a town—not as big, though. I *do* understand how it is. People get into little ruts, don't know how to live, really. I mean *really* live in a big way! That's why I got out. Don't get me wrong, I like these towns. But in college I learned how to make my way around in the male world, as an equal."

He merely remained silent, watching, waiting. She continued with a light bubbly laugh.

"Well, a girl with brains knows men and women are fairly much alike. We all have the same emotional problems—egos that want caressing—desires that are fairly equal. Now...you see what I'm getting at?"

"Not quite," David lied, wanting to change the subject, but not quite knowing how.

"Well, some women shove their so-called superiority...or so-called equality...into a man's face. And some *are* brainier as there are women who are more attractive than their male counterparts. But that goes both ways. People are people and there are different degrees of superiority, not limited to any one sex."

It was almost amusing seeing her work on him. She wasn't being obvious so much as skillful, even if somewhat off the wall.

After taking a sip of her drink, she continued. "Now, take the two of us. We are fairly equal, I would say, both in our positions in the business world and in our physical at-

90

tractiveness. I mean, you're a looker. And I don't underestimate my own appeal to men. Now it would be foolish of me to attempt to prove what is obvious, wouldn't it? Neither of us would be in this...well, hotel room...together, if we weren't considered by our own firms as equal. So, what would there be to prove?"

A short quiet followed that, then she requested, almost huskily: "How about more champagne?"

David took the bottle and walked over to the bed. Standing over her, he could see deep down between her breasts, a sight that was intended to create a very animal response. She gazed up, lips almost pouting.

"Do you mind," she inquired, "if I ask you a question?"

"I guess not."

"Are you afraid of me?"

David felt as if he had been slapped in the face.

"Why...*should* I be afraid of you?" David managed to laugh.

"Oh, I don't know. You seem distant. Ever since you stepped into the room. I—well, it was almost as if you resented me—no, not quite that! More as if you didn't *trust* me." She smiled as if nervous.

"Hardly. But we are kinda on two difference sides of a business negotiation. And—"

"Oh, now, David!" she laughed. "We don't have to be that competitive about it. Do we? Can't we be at least friendly about it all? Business is business, but that doesn't mean we have to be all business. Nor not at least on friendly terms."

"I guess not," he managed, though still somewhat cautious.

"You still sound hesitant." She continued to look up at him, with a generous, inviting smile on her face. "Well, all of this *could* look pretty seductive, I suppose."

She made a sweep of the room with her arm.

Her eyes met his, now honestly brazen, fully aware of what she had said and making no effort to suggest that the idea was unappealing to her. A smoldering fire danced deep in her eyes, bright, hot with invitation. "If I'd known what

91

you were like, I might have done just that."

David backed away, the bottle of champagne in one hand and his empty glass in the other.

"But," she continued, "this is just my normal standard of living. Hopefully it doesn't bother you. I like nice things. And I don't believe in being coy about it. And what I'm all about is...well, simply a woman who does what she can to make a living and enjoy life to the hilt. So to speak. We only live once and we all better make the most of it while we can. Life is terribly short. Don't you agree?

When he said nothing, she stood. "Well, anyway, we can't have you feeling uncomfortable with me. Nonetheless I'm a single woman who keeps her very casual, without strings attached. And as to the...personal side...well...I'm no prude, to be blunt about it." She laughed, shrugged, then offered: "As you know, a career woman can't afford to equate sex with love and marriage; or even with an emotional attachment, if she wants to remain on top. I don't plan on ever getting married, simply because it is too much fun living the way I do."

She paused, then with an apparently startled intake of breath, exclaimed: "I don't know what made me say that."

Then in a smaller, softer voice: "I'm sorry. But, to be blunt...you're somewhat overwhelming!"

"And you're somewhat outspoken," he offered, somewhat defensively.

She was half turned away from him, but now she looked up into his eyes. "I'm actually harmless, really." Her index finger circled on his shoulder, as if pensive, thoughtful. "I merely find my pleasures where they come along. When I see an attractive male I wonder what it would be like with him. It's only natural. A body does react...a girl can't help herself, David. And you are one hunk!"

Freda's words were throaty, her eyes half-lidded, her mouth moist, half-parted, only inches from his. There was that glazed, hungry expression on her face like he had seen on Pat's and Connie's when they were about to let him take them to bed.

Suddenly David wondered how she had managed to get the conversation around to this level of sensuality so

92

quickly. Here they were, total strangers, and she came right out and laid it on the line.

"I'm not the kind of woman who can hold back...her emotions, or her feelings...David," Freda half-moaned, suddenly closer, her body just lightly touching his. "I'd just love knowing you better. That's a simple fact of life. And damned silly to not admit the truth! And I don't want complications! Just casual pleasures...to be honest. I don't cling, can't afford more than momentary connections with attractive male partners. Is that blunt enough?!"

There it was, a bold, direct, open offer. No strings.

David felt wild excitement. His mind screamed: screw her and forget it. Nobody would really know except the two of them.

Suddenly Freda's lips touched his, her arms slipped around his neck, her body pressed aggressively close, hips squirming slightly. He felt her tongue run along his lips and suddenly he wasn't thinking much about anything other than her nearness, the hot fire hurting him, he was hard as a rock.

Then her tongue was deep in his mouth, searching, caressing, passionate in its greedy need. Her thigh pressed hard between his legs.

Just as abruptly, Freda pushed away, turned from him, said: "I'm sorry, David. I know you're the kind of man who's loyal to your wife. I just couldn't help it. I was simply overwhelmed. I'm single. I'm a woman who takes her men as they come along. I shouldn't have done that to you. Not fair. Please forgive me. Will you? Please?"

Her voice was so pleading and childlike, that emotion struck him deep.

"I shouldn't have done that. I know my rep suggests I'm some kind of evil seductress who'll do anything to close a deal. Well that's not really true. I'm just a woman. And I have needs. And sometimes things just happen. You're really an attractive man. And I've had a tough day, and I'm feeling a little of the wine bubbling in my head. And well, this is a rather seductive setting, I'll admit. But I didn't mean it that way. Just that...oh, darn. I'm making a fool of myself. Can we just start all over?"

She pleaded with her eyes and was damningly con-

93

vincing.

All at once David felt protective towards Freda; as he might feel toward any woman who attracted him in a strong physical way. For a moment he began to think that maybe he had misjudged her; maybe she had been merely expressing her honest feelings; an overwhelming desire for him.

That certainly wasn't beyond belief. People did meet strangers and suddenly lust for one another. And she was one stunner.

At that point, just as he was about to step forward and put his arm around her shoulder, there was a gentle knock on the door.

Freda whipped around. "Oh, the dinner. I'd forgotten."

There was just the touch of relief in her voice, as if she'd been suddenly rescued from an awkward situation. "We better settle down to more serious matters, right?"

She seemed in control of herself; almost *too* much control, David noticed, as she moved to the door to open it.

As food was brought in on a serving table, David had a chance to recover from the little play that had just taken place. As he reconstructed it, everything seemed too pat, too well played out by Freda. She had taken over from the moment he stepped into the room, not giving him a chance to breathe, leaving no air for thinking out his next response before she slipped into another act. Every word had led to one destination: his arms, a passionate kiss, a step back to bring out his full male response.

And the woman had known the meal was coming. Had it all been masterfully planned out, timed to gain a powerful advantage over him, right from the start? She'd made a brazen, bold play, set the scene, a tease right within the proper limits, timed just right, before the food arrived to interrupt any further action in a seductive direction, at this point, at least. Now he, the marked man, would have time to consider just where things could likely end. She was stunning, a seductive trap dressed to kill all resistance. And after what had just taken place could any man sit across the dinner table from her without wanting to take up her offer of sex with no strings attached.

94

Yes, sure, of course.

In college, after the summer affair with Connie, he had known a woman called Helen, about three years older than himself; dark-haired, big boned and sexy in every way. She was much like Freda. She worked as a waitress and he learned to know her too damned well. The first time they had dated after her working hours when she'd suggested they go to her place, Helen had come on fast and strong the moment her apartment door was closed. She was in his arms, her whole body kissing his, lips open, mouth almost sucking his tongue out of place. Her hands were all over his back, one pressed into his buttocks; the other reached between his legs. She moaned in his ear: "I'm hot for you!"

The phone rang, and she grabbed his hand, dragged him bodily after her. Picking up the receiver, she said "Hello," while taking his hand and dipping down, so that it was possible to pull her skirt up. With her urging, he was all but forced to peel down her panties. She then directed his fingers while carrying on a very business-like kind of conversation on the phone. Her hips twisted and reacted. Suddenly she had hung up the phone and said: "Give me a real working over, love, I'll take care of you real good!"

There was never anything subtle about this woman and he dated her for some time because no man could turn down such a piece of action.

She had been divorced and needed sex in big, large doses. She never played games about it.

She had also revealed sharp changes of moods, much like Freda, being all business when she worked, all animal sexual-whore in private. She simply liked sex and couldn't get enough of it.

But Freda had pulled another trick on him.

She used a simple theory: First get a guy to like you, after hitting him with a highly-charged orgastically sexual impact, then make him understand you as a person and after that, feel protective towards you.

David watched her as the waiters served the food, realizing how Freda was so much like that waitress; all sex—like an orgasmic female creature, turned on by a man, maybe *any* man!

95

Once the waiters had left, Freda's eyes softly searched his.

"I'm sorry about the pass." She was close enough to embrace. "Nasty business, that. I mean, not very business-like of me. You know. But. Heck. I'm just a woman, and you're a man and, quite frankly under other circumstances I suppose we might..." Her body made a little move, ever so subtle, that seemed to almost point to the bed behind her, yet didn't change her position facing him. "Well, you know...down to business, I suppose. Dinner, first, to feed our bodies for the action to follow!"

Christ, he thought, *what was that supposed to mean?*

"Any way, David, please just chalk it down to a lonely woman's foolishness. I just find you attractive. And I was out of line. Sorry."

Now in control of the situation, David casually stated: "I'm really flattered, Freda."

She seemed to lean towards him, as if about to make her most open and sensual play. Her lips hung open, moist, glistening, her breasts seemed to heave against the cocktail gown.

"But, like you said, I am very much in love with my wife. If I were free like you—it's always nice to know you're still desirable to the opposite sex." Yet he was feeling somewhat drunk with the seething desire ebbing up through his body at the very nearness her. Literally he wanted to totally dive in and smother himself within the woman's naked embrace. He couldn't get his mind off that raw desire.

The dinner was excellent and generous. By the time they had finished eating, the champagne bottle was empty. The dinner conversation stayed on a general, impersonal level, covering the world situation and the Wall Street ups and downs, but never anything concerning their business or each other. Yet the erotic background was stunningly obvious.

Once finished, Freda offered: "I'll order some cocktails, while you get your papers ready to show me."

There was no question about his agreeing or disagreeing with this suggestion. She glided toward the hotel phone in her sensual way and sat down on the bed. That walk

96

was designed to drive a man's desire wildly up a couple of notches—animal, sexual, cat-like.

David busied himself with his briefcase. By the time drinks had been ordered, he was prepared to present his offer to Freda. She motioned him to the bed beside her. The businesslike movement of her hand, the serious expression on her face left no room for doubt that now was not the time for seductive passes.

Freda pulled a glass case from the nightstand. As he sat down beside her, she put on a pair of very businesslike horn-rimmed glasses, which came to a point at each side.

"Now," she announced, taking his work-sheet in hand, putting it on her lap. "Let's see what you have here."

One quick sweep of the page and Freda laughed. "You gotta be kidding, fellow."

Her eyes shot up to his. "These figures are way out of line. We can't do business on these terms, *period!* That's that. Better go back and talk it over with the rest of your boys. I don't want to waste my time or yours with these!"

She handed the paper back to David, stood and faced him like some tall demon goddess, hands on hips, feet slightly spread apart. Her wide, well-formed hips only a foot from his face. Erotic, tempting.

David was taken aback by her sudden change from seductress to hard-nosed businesswoman. Her eyes narrowed, coldness had changed them to stone emerald.

She had him on the defensive again, and David felt at a momentary loss for words.

"Mr. Carter, you can't honestly be serious about this? A sixty percent profit."

"What makes you think it's a sixty per-center?" David now managed in an even voice, almost able to ignore her blatant visual sexuality.

"Don't take me for a fool. I do know what the costs allowed would be. Sixty percent is merely a close guess. It might be more, for all I know. But we aren't in the business of being taken for suckers. I don't come into a business meeting without all the figures in my mind. Just because I'm a woman, don't get the idea you can push me around." Then a little more softly; "Business is one thing, David, personal is personal. What happened before dinner was Freda, the woman—*that* I can't control. But business I *can* control! And I'm a control freak. My company just won't stand for this, do you understand?"

David now stood, fully aroused, his anger seething under the control now taking effect. Never before had he known such an outspoken, hard negotiator. No man would have talked that way. Only a woman like Freda could get away with it and only then because of her sex. And what sex! He was aware of a hard pressure of an erection against his pants.

"Look, Miss Hendricks, I'm not a fool, either. We have figures, too. We know exactly who you'll sell these plates to and for what kind of money! *We* aren't in the business of manufacturing for pleasure. We have to make a profit."

"A profit, yes. A robbery, no!" she spat out in a cold voice. Yet everything, even anger, seemed sexy about Freda.

"Everybody has a right to their share of profit, Miss Hendricks! And—" He broke off, said more quietly, "and I would like to go over these figures with you in a more calm manner. Maybe we can come to a better understanding of one another."

She smiled then. "Okay, David. And none of this Mister and Miss thing, right? Sorry." Her voice was soft husky sex.

She placed a hand on each of his shoulders. "Forgive me? I sometimes forget myself."

The touch was almost too much! It was electric fire.

He felt the impulse to sweep her into his arms, but fought it back. "Okay. Now let's get down to business. Okay?"

Just then a knock sounded on the door.

"Come on in," Freda called, twisting around.

She smiled seductively at David.

A waiter entered the room, carrying a small silver tray. Freda had ordered three double Martinis and three double Scotches and Cream.

David was surprised about the drinks she had for him. "How'd you know?"

98

She merely shrugged. "Trade secrets. My business is to know everything possible about a man with whom I'm going to do business."

"Then the wife bit and the child thing—"

"Were simple addition." She considered him, lips pouting. "Simple addition, considering the report I received about you yesterday afternoon." She smiled knowingly. "You have a sister-in-law, a Connie Lewis, staying with you. She was an old girl friend of yours. Yesterday you had lunch together."

He felt and looked stunned. "Christ!"

Freda shrugged. "All in a day's work, David."

She lifted a Martini, nodded to him. "To a good business arrangement between the two of us.'

After taking a stiff swallow of the Martini, Freda sat down on the bed, patted the space next to her. "Now, down to business, I'll listen to you, then you listen to me, okay? Friends to the end."

"Okay."

How her words had been heavy with sex, he realized.

For the next hour they exchanged ideas about the proposed contract, but neither of them could come to a total agreement without talking to their superiors. By the time they were finished with their discussion, Freda was on her third Martini and David just finishing off his last Scotch and cream.

"Well, that does it, I guess," Freda announced, taking his papers and putting them on the nightstand. She turned and faced him. Her manner changed, she relaxed, smiled warmly. "You know, you are fun to do business with. A real fireball!"

She looked tenderly at him. With one swift movement her right hand removed the glasses, placed them on his papers.

"How about a night-cap?" She leaned over, opened the bottom drawer of the nightstand, and pulled out a bottle of expensive Scotch. "You can hardly turn me down, since I went to a lot of trouble to get this *especially* for you."

David noticed the bottle with pleasure. *Chivas Regal, Royal Salute.* Impressive, expensive and one of the best aged

99

Scotches on the market.

She opened the bottle and filled their glasses. "You know, David, I think I'm going to like doing business with you. You're honest, outspoken. You aren't afraid to snap back. That's what a *man* should do! I might be a woman, but I don't pull any punches, either when it comes to business. I don't mind admitting that sometimes I get a little too hard—but that's my job, to use every weapon possible! Some men hesitate to snap back. But...well, I guess you took notice of how I shout it out!"

She laughed lightly, lips parting over even white teeth.

David smiled, sipped the Scotch, commented about how smooth it was, and then said: "You *are* a hard head."

Freda leaned close, touched his cheek. "I'm a woman, too. A soft, yielding woman, with womanly desires. Don't confuse the two parts of me." After gazing into his eyes for a long time, haunting depths of sexual hunger burning brightly in her eyes, she said: "You are a dear, David."

Her voice was low, husky. "A real, attractive, sexy dear."

Without warning Freda came closer, kissed him. Then her left hand slipped around his neck as her lips parted. The point of her tongue played teasingly along his lips. He felt the soft pressure of her fleshy breasts against him.

That contact, the nearness of her fired through him like wild needles. All he could think of was surrendering to her obvious offer—knowing it would end with the two of them nakedly exploring one another to a final explosive orgasm. He wanted to fight her off, to push her away, but couldn't do anything but respond.

Helpless, David felt his mouth open under the insistent urging of her tongue, which quickly shot deep past his teeth the moment he gave it entrance. The dam of resistance burst free.

The drinks were already dizzily swimming in his brain, and he felt like a man sinking into a violent whirlpool.

His hand automatically found her breasts, which were naked under the satin cloth. She moaned, her lips moved from his, ran down his cheek, worried his ear.

100

He was suddenly floating in a wild sea of erotic need, thrilling to the texture of the woman, unable to think of anything other than totally possessing her flesh. Her hands were caressing all over him, insistently, stunningly thrilling.

Then he felt her reach between his legs and wondered how she had so skillfully managed to nakedly expose him, without his realizing it. She moaned in his ear: "Oh, David, I love it! Just feeling you like this, it's ... lovely!"

Helpless, David felt himself pushed onto the bed, as Freda's breathe burned hot against him. "Oh, you lovely man...beautiful—man!" Then a terrible, anguished sigh uttered from him as he felt her soft moist lips and tongue envelop him.

How sanity returned, he didn't know.

David came to his senses as Freda's lips left him. He sat up, determined to stop her before it was too late.

But Freda reached out, her hands like soft, velvet claws, powerfully urged him towards her. He felt momentarily helpless, driven by such overwhelming desire that he couldn't resist. She pulled him down onto the bed. They lay side by side, straining together, their bodies squirmed against one another. He found his hand helplessly running up over her nylon-covered legs, until it pushed the skirt of the gown high upon her thighs. He touched soft, warm naked flesh above the stockings and a wild beating pain rush all over him.

He had to stop!

But couldn't. A basic part of him didn't want to stop.

How he had to possess this woman's body right then. Her skin was velvet, the thighs hot like fire. It was impossible to stop. Her hand still teased him between the legs, thrilling stroking, caressing, the finger tips driving waves of need to keep him hurting more and more—they were already beyond the point of stopping.

Suddenly her right hand reached back, unzipped her dress. An instant later she exposed one large naked breast, which arched up in an eager surge for a voluptuous kiss.

He felt hypnotized. That supple mound of white, dotted by its large rigid nipple was suddenly moving closer as her hands closed on his shoulders, drawing him downwards.

David's head was throbbing, his body hurt with harsh desire. He looked at her breast, firm, the nipple so tight that it seemed to be screaming with want.

Freda's hands found his neck, urged his head even closer to that brimming breast.

"Kiss me," she moaned.

Something snapped in David's mind, so sharply that it seemed as if all his nerves had been jerked out of his body. The bright heat of passion shot away, the violent fire that had strangled him now flickered out.

There was something cold-blooded, calculated, even if very real, in the way she had come after him. He didn't doubt her sexual hunger, but he couldn't deal with the reality of what was happening. Something cold chilled down his spine.

"Freda...no!" David said unemotionally, in a loud voice. "I can't."

How he managed to force himself away from her, David was not quite sure. All at once he was standing, watching Freda, who casually rearranged her dress as if nothing had happened. She sat up, zipped the gown back into place.

David now knew why it was impossible to make love to Freda. It would be cold sex and only sex.

No, that wasn't enough for David. No sexual cop-outs. No sex just for kicks!

Pat might never know but he would know. The hurt was not worth the pleasure. With Connie, he admitted, it might be different. David had little doubt that it would be impossible to turn Connie down under the same circumstances. But that would be different because he had loved Connie and believed he still did.

Freda stood, stared at him for a moment then said: "Like I always say, David, you can't blame a girl for trying. You turn me on! I'm sorry. *Really* am. You're a swell husband—but a damned bastard!"

She laughed, embarrassedly. "You really shouldn't let a girl go all that far without stopping her before it gets...well, too close to the main event. I'm quite hot all over!"

102

"I'm sorry, Freda, about that. It's just that Pat—"

"Sure. A girl is lucky to have a husband who loves her *that* much!" She seemed slightly flustered, nervous, in less control of herself than she had been all evening.

David felt sudden need to make her understand. "It's not you, believe me—it wasn't easy."

Freda cut him short with a shake of her head. "Don't think you have to make excuses. I've been around long enough, known enough men and know myself. I'm not hurt emotionally when a man is loyal to his wife. It only hurts physically. But a girl gets over that quickly enough."

David didn't know what to say about that while he fumbled with his briefcase, collecting his papers. "Well, I guess I better—"

"Tell that wife of yours how lucky she is."

Freda briskly helped him leave by immediately moving to the door. "I'll be in contact sometime tomorrow. Okay?"

"Okay."

Once outside, David began shaking. Suddenly he wondered what kind of a fool he was. She had been his. There was nothing to hold him back. Except his love for Pat. But not for the reasons Freda had pointed out.

David felt cheap and sick with himself. If Connie hadn't returned from Hollywood, he could have walked away from Freda, believing that his love for Pat was too great to cheat on her. But David knew this to be far from the truth.

All he could think of was making love to Connie.

* * * * * * *

Once Freda knew that David Carter was gone for good, she took the glass in her hand, threw it furiously against the wall. Her hands hungrily clutched at her crotch, her whole body churning with desperate need.

"Damn that bastard!" she half screamed. "I'm hurting hot!"

A moment later she picked up the hotel phone, asked: "Where can a girl get a man!"

103

The clerk's voice came from the receiver with a light edge of surprise. "What is it you want?"

"If I was a *man,* you'd know where to get a *girl!*" Freda snapped, angrily. "Fifty dollars for immediate service, for your own pocket. Got the idea? I mean *right now!*"

She slammed down the receiver. The way she felt right then it didn't matter what kind of stud serviced her. She'd screw a bedpost, if that was all she could find and do it willingly.

Desperately furious inwardly at failing to get David Carter to complete the act with her, Freda angrily stripped her body naked. She lay on the bed, hands between her legs, caressing, burning so hot that it was impossible to control the naked need.

In her life she'd had enough experience with hotels to know how to pull strings and get a man, *fast!* A clerk, a bell-hop; they'd find somebody to play stud for a paying guest. And she was quick to always make it clear she tipped big. When a big spender was around, hotel staffs snapped-to! Fast!

She couldn't have been laying there for more than a few minutes before knock sounded on the door.

"Come in," she demanded.

A key slipped into the lock, then a bellhop entered the room, eyes large as he saw her naked form on the bed.

"Close the damned door, you stupid fool!" she cursed. When the young man did so, she almost screamed in agony: "Get those pants off...come over here to me, love. And do it fast before I burst!"

Like a zombie the man stepped to the bed, naked from the waist down.

She looked at him, irritated. "Can't you get hard, just looking?"

Before he could say anything, Freda swung her legs over the side of the bed, reached out between his thighs, cursed: "I'll get you fucking hard!"

Her fingers pulled on his limp manhood, then her lips covered the soft crown. She knew how to get an erection fast, and that's what she needed. With lips and tongue, using her hand on his testicles, Freda fairly devoured the man until

104

he was as stiff as it was possible to make him.

"Now," she said, releasing him, "you shove that in me good!"

Lying back, legs parted, she trembled as he mounted her. Then a gasp of heavenly pleasure shot through her whole body.

Her hips thrust up and down, as her body experienced easy orgasms, exhausting itself under him.

Afterwards, Freda took a fifty-dollar bill and handed it to the man, saying: "You did a good job, honey."

He tried to reject the money, but she simply shoved it back into his hand, saying: "Take it. I got more out of this than you did. Just keep that damned mouth of yours quiet. That's what the money is for! Understand?"

He nodded, starting to leave.

"If you do like I say, maybe we'll try it again, okay?"

He nodded and left, as dazed as he had come.

Freda lighted a cigarette and considered David Carter in a more serious, less lustfully upset manner.

She had needed somebody like the young man to clear her head. Now to the serious business.

She was going to get him, but good; next time around. There were tricks she knew that would make any man spring into action. If she had to rape him against his will, she'd put the man in a submissive position to make him helpless in closing the deal with her.

A slow, cruel smile played on her sensual lips as she considered David. "Yes, my young man," she thought with a sense of pleasure, "the next time, I'll have you on the floor on your hands and knees, begging to screw me! And then, you won't be so damned hard-nosed about making a good deal! Little old Freda knows men and a good frontal attack will drive even little old you beyond control. You son-of-a-bitching bastard!"

CHAPTER EIGHT

Pat was sewing some of her son's stockings, which had been ripped with holes. Connie was across the room, a drink of whiskey sitting beside her. For some time neither of them had talked.

Connie felt horny as hell. How she needed a man, almost any man in one way. Especially David. It was his fault. She hadn't realized that the wild spark between them hadn't even simmered down in the least. It still lay there like some explosive power keg. Then, to top matters a call from Harvey Peterson a little while before had sparked her to a further needy high. Yet she really didn't want to be with that man; partly because any such involvement might get back to David; the last thing she wanted. For more than three weeks she'd been without any sexual outlet and the desire for David had brought on a strong need. That was all a surprise. After 11 years and the flame seethed like a hot coal inside her. Sparked alive by the very presence of the man in the same room.

In Reno she'd been gambling at the blackjack table next to a man about her age. They talked. Then later left the table, had some drinks together. She was on the make and it was made obvious to him. She couldn't even remember his name. But he was large in every way. And she wanted to enjoy what he could offer a woman.

It was one hell of a good orgy-scene. One she hadn't experienced for a very long time. They drank a lot of booze. But that didn't stop them from literally feasting on one another. The man had kept her going all night long, then again in the morning totally wiping her out. Strangely she had very little memory of the details, only the fact that they'd ex-

106

hausted each other.

It was the kind of scene she needed, right now!

Connie realized something would have to give and soon—or she'd go out of her mind!

Pat asked: "You like Harvey?" The question was guarded.

"He's all right." Connie felt annoyed by the question.

"But you'll go out with him?" The voice accused, as if Pat were implying something somewhat questionable.

"He's nice. Maybe." Connie snapped, feeling bitchy. "What kind of question is that?"

"Well, you don't sound like you really like him," Pat pointed out, looking up from her sewing.

"What's that got to do with it? He's a man. He's okay. I have nothing against him—not yet, anyway," Connie laughed, thinking how her statement could be taken two ways. "I could go out with him, simply because he's there."

There had been something in her sister's manner that suggested slight disapproval of going out with a man who didn't really attract her. And it would happen with Harvey, simply because he was so obviously interested in sex. Even if she felt uncomfortable about somebody too close to David.

She laughed: "I'd probably screw him silly, too!"

Pat stared at Connie, eyes wide. "You're kidding!"

"Why not?" Connie delighted in her sister's surprise. It was so Small Town, USA. She felt the violent urge to really shock Pat.

"But...sleeping with a man you hardly even know. How can you even think of such a thing?" Pat had put her sewing on her lap, ignoring it.

"Look, sister mine—the first thing a man and woman have together—and in fact that *only* thing, in the beginning—is the subconscious desire to bluntly fuck away. Only children delude themselves into thinking otherwise. They try to tell themselves that it is romantic love. It is all about glands screaming with over-stimulation. Grow up! Adults seek each other out because they want companionship and they want it not only for verbal conversation but also in the wee hours of the night—screwing in bed. Face it. Fucking is fun! You don't have to like a guy to be hungry for him—all

107

he has to do is be physically attractive. If he knows how to deliver, super! You're in for a thrill. In the dark, Pat, it really doesn't matter who's with you, just so a man can do the right things to your body."

"Oh, Connie, how can you talk that way? I'm surprised! Sometimes I don't even think I know you. You never were like that—when we were kids."

"Well, we aren't kids, now, honey. We're adults. And I've been away for a very long time. Things change."

"You seem like a stranger!"

"We *are* strangers, in a way, Pat. Years have gone by—and those years have changed the both of us." Connie smiled warmly. "But we *are* sisters. That's the nice thing about it. You're married, a mother—I'm a single girl on the make. I'll admit it. A woman who hits thirty knows about life and sex and knows how her body has certain physical hungers, for food, drink and sex. I'd be a bloody fool to sit here and tell you that I didn't like sex. And damned if I wouldn't sleep with a good looking stud who excited me. Just because there is some kind of moral code that nobody in their right mind really follows to the letter after they're over twenty-one?"

Connie lighted a cigarette. "I sometimes just need a male animal pleasuring me!"

"You're horrible!" Pat laughed nervously.

"Why? Just because I admit the truth to myself? Just because I'm honest about life? Sex is a very big part of it. Not so much when you're married—strangely enough—as it is when you are single. I've been through both routes. I'll tell you right now that single people go out with one another for one basic reason: loneliness and well, a good fuck—and don't kid yourself! Some girls sit on their hands and say they wouldn't touch a man without wedding bells—at least the ding-donging in the offing. Prudes are nothing but liars to themselves. A smart person faces the truth, lives a life that takes in all the body hungers. Mind, spirit *and*...groin!" She really felt like being bitchy bold and not edited the more natural, blunt terms. Pat would be shocked to hear her talk crudely; Small Town, U.S.A. Right down to the tight-lipped morality. "And don't kid yourself, there's plenty of action all

108

around you here."

"Oh, Con, I know…in fact there's a couple down the street who are rather blunt about having an open marriage. Everybody knows they sleep out on one another."

"Oh, God, Pat. I hope they aren't *sleeping* out!"

"You know what I mean."

"Of course. Sleeping out. In a sleepy town of hypocritical morons. Sleeping my ass! Fucking out, is more like it!" She laughed at that, delighted in the shock-value it had on Pat.

"Connie. Really!"

"Well, why don't you just come out and say it like it is?"

"Not necessary. You know what I mean."

"Fucking around with other partners! Right?"

"Do you have to?" Pat demanded, voice quite annoyed, as her eyes snapped up to meet Connie's.

"Why not? Sex is normal. Every day stuff. Everybody does it, married or not, in and out of that holy bond. I don't know a man who hasn't slept out on his wife. And a lot of women I've known wouldn't think twice about doing the same thing if given the chance."

"Well I haven't. And I really don't believe David has, either." The words sounded angry, and somewhat uncertain. "I'm sure of that. David is loyal and—"

"Any man will if he's under the right kind of pressure. And most of them do at some time or other in their lives. It isn't a world-shattering thing and a smart woman understands it isn't a real threat to her marriage, either. Stupid ones use it as an excuse to get out of a questionable relationship. So? We're all human with needs. And it isn't immoral just so long as you aren't trying to hurt others. But— and believe me, I learned this lesson over and over again— you gotta think of *number one,* first! When I speak about not hurting others, I mean that a man and woman will seek each other out and screw like hell, but not in the middle of Hollywood and Vine, in broad daylight. They go off someplace nice and cozy for their romantic interludes. Bang, bang! Now wasn't that great, honey?"

She laughed, hoping that might break the chill and

109

was relieved to see Pat relax a little.

"You *are* terrible," Pat laughed, this time with bright humor. "I don't think I've talked quite that boldly about sex with you before."

Connie nodded. "Mom and Dad seemed like well, they didn't know what sex was all about. I learned differently, though. When I was in my teens I came upon them one evening—you were out on an all-night sleeping party with some of your girl friends. I'd gotten mad at my date and came home early. I don't know who was more surprised, me or the folks. They were in the living room, Mom sitting, Dad on his hands and knees between her legs, kissin' her up like you wouldn't believe! Mom wasn't totally naked. Her bra was off and the dress just barely hanging by threads to her hips and Dad going down on—"

"Please," Pat blushed. "I don't want to hear." Connie laughed and it sounded hard and cruel.

"Okay. I'll keep it off the folks. But believe me...people will do all kinds of things."

Pat hesitated, then asked: "I suppose you've had … well… many men...I mean...that you've gone out with a lot of men...well, you..."

"There have been enough," Connie mused, tickled by her sister's obvious curiosity. Like so many women with little experience with men, Pat was fascinated by Connie's admissions.

"How *could* you?" Pat cried, almost with humor, but also with an edge of tension hiding real annoyance. "My own sister!"

"God, Pat. I'm just a woman. And I've had some very tough times. I told you some about that. And they play a hard game out there. And I mean hard in every way. Down and dirty hard!"

"You make that sound cheap."

"Nothing cheap about it. They had their hard little problems and they let the ladies solve them. Some are nice about it; I'll admit that. But there are others who will be rather crude and bold and simply look at you, saying, 'Maybe you'd be good for the part, but why should I give it to you? There are a lot of hot chicks willing to put out for a part like this. What are you willing to do for it?' And that's a nice pitch for sex. Some have just said: 'Why not come over here and let me really get to know you better!' Or the real shocker can be: 'You want the part, then fuck me for it!'"

"You're kidding?"

"Not at all. Most are, though, nice guys who may hint around a bit, flirt, or simply be complimentary. Some are bluntly arms-distance, no touchie you, no touchie them. But there's a lot of the ol' casting couch being offered up and some girls are just circulated from one to another, sometimes even getting parts to keep them hooked. But … it can be very nasty business, if you don't play it smart."

"And you…"

"I did my best."

"Did you…let them…do…well, take advantage of you?"

"How could I keep *from* it? In the world out there a girl learns fast to roll with the punches. There were times when I could have...well, there were some men that I—quite frankly—didn't like!"

Pat started to say something then shook her head from side to side.

"Well, don't be surprised. Sometimes a girl will do anything to just survive! I'd do anything to survive, and I have survived! Some events in my past life aren't too pretty. Things are set up against the career girl—I mean the starlets! It goes the same with the men. You get into a trap—well, you make it yourself, I guess. But, struggling to get parts in the movies, gigs in nightclubs, puts you out of circulation for normal every-day jobs. When you say you haven't worked in the last couple of years in an office job, they'll sometimes maybe consider hiring you pat time at *$200 a month!* That's not enough to keep you in make-up!"

Connie stabbed out her cigarette, took a sip of the whiskey, and then lighted another cigarette. "So...when some slob offers a good part or gig, you fuck him, if that's part of a solid business agreement."

Pat's eyes flashed. "David was the only one with me, you know."

"No, I didn't," Connie lied, almost laughing. But she

111

managed to keep her face straight.

"We've never talked about Dave, have we? I mean, the fact that both of us went out with him."

"What's there to talk about?" Connie took another sip of her drink, suddenly feeling very smug fighting back the urge to reveal in blunt, vulgar terms how it really *had* been with David and her.

"Well, you did know him, first. I mean—"

"Yes, I did know him first!" Connie admitted, feeling brutal and surprised how much she enjoyed it. She was high now, and her thoughts ran along the road of least resistance. She felt a hard bitterness toward Pat and the world in general when she realized how all of David could be hers if she hadn't gone to Hollywood.

"You *did* leave town, Connie," Pat countered as if that explained everything. Then more quickly, as if nervous about making her understand, "I didn't really think anything would come of it at first. I was...well curious."

Connie felt sudden defensiveness. "Curious about what?"

"Well...you were fairly popular and had the pick of men—and I always wondered what you saw in David Carter."

Acid was thick in Connie s voice, now. "You found out fast enough!"

Pat didn't say anything to that. Her eyes returned to the sewing. After a while she stated:

"He's a fine man, Connie. A good husband. We have shared a lot of happy years together."

It sounded as if Pat was not only trying to defend herself but at the same time protect her marriage. Connie immediately felt panic because her own thoughts generated a real threat to Pat.

"I guess you are making Dave very happy, Pat," Connie managed to admit in a controlled voice. "I'm happy for both of you."

Pat stared up at her, relief showing on her slender features. She smiled shyly. "I'm glad you feel that way. I've always felt...well, that you might have...misunderstood or felt resentment. Oh, I don't know—just a feeling."

112

"Well, rest assured, sis, your big sister is tickled pink to have Dave as part of the family. The fact that we dated some has nothing to do with you and him. Or you and me. It's in the past. There was nothing between us, anyway," she lied. What a pleasure it would be to tell Pat the detailed truth.

Pat hesitated before saying: "I always thought...well, that he was quite serious about you, back then when you were dating."

Connie forced a laugh. "Don't be silly. Puppy love brought on by youthful sexual hungers. We both were young, innocent and childish! Nothing more. And in any case, after all, he fell in love with you and married you. What more do you want?"

You stupid bitch! She added silently.

"Nothing. I just want Dave. He's my whole life. And our son, of course."

They were silent for a long time after that, then Pat asked: "What was your life really like in Hollywood? All those years...I've wondered. Now...what you said before—"

Connie shrugged. "Nothing interesting, really. Had a lot of tough breaks; that's all. If things had been going well I wouldn't be here now. And I guess I'll have to go back soon enough. I know that my life can hardly be limited to this small town. I've...well, I don't know—don't want to talk about it right now."

Pat looked relieved.

In the quiet that followed, Connie's thoughts drifted back to her first years in Hollywood. It had been damned bitter, hard and an eye-opener.

First there were the desperate jobs as a waitress, just to make ends meet. The ends had met plenty of times. She was lonely. Men seemed to think they could make blunt passes; they got away with it at times, simply because she liked sex a lot. Once she'd screwed a man silly in his car, straddling his hips.

Then she'd roomed with a series of young girls her own age to keep expenses down to a point where it was possible to go to drama school. Some wild parties had taken place during that time. She'd done just about everything. She and her roommate had a number of wild parties. Once with

113

several men in a kind of mutually shared wonderful "gang bang" that went on all night. But the next day she'd felt cheap and dirty about it.

Always there was the next day to face.

Then the first Lesbian scene that had taught her another way to enjoy intimacy.

It was a dark-haired Latin girl about twenty-six, brash, bold and a little too aggressive. They'd had some pretty good parties with men, so there had never been any reason to believe the girl was bisexual.

At first Connie thought the aggressiveness was merely a normal hardened attitude of a career girl. Then one night, when Connie came home from an interview with a night-club owner who had hired her for a couple of weeks as band vocalist, the girl insisted they celebrate in their apartment together, getting smashed.

In the beginning Connie had no idea what was about to happen. They had roomed together for only a few months but filled with enough male-sexual activity to prove both of them quite man-hungry.

Well, drinks followed drinks, the girl suggested they dance. "I feel like dancing and there's nobody here but us girls!"

Without giving Connie a chance to think about it, she turned on the radio and started dancing with her, taking a strong lead. She wore a flame-red sweater and now Connie noticed that she wasn't wearing a bra. The heavy breasts, unlike many Latin girls, were firm, well shaped and youthful. The dance seemed strangely. She attempted to keep her distance but it was impossible. After several dances, the girl suddenly announced she was very hot and pulled off her sweater.

"Why don't we both get naked?" was the next suggestion. "It's sorta nice to be naked, no confining clothes, freedom of body, natural as we were born."

Connie didn't really see anything wrong with that. They were both women, and she did suddenly feel a little warm. Checking the heaters, Connie noticed the temperature was well above eighty degrees.

"Don't you think we should cut down the setting?"

114

she wondered.

"Why bother? If we're naked it won't make any difference." She caressed her breasts as if warming herself.

"Cold, already?" Connie laughed.

"No, just feels good!"

Connie was surprised by that, but again did not get the idea. It had never occurred to her to think about this woman making love to another woman. Especially because they'd had some real wild sex-parties in their apartment. If Connie had ever considered the idea of female homosexuals it would have been to equate them with their male counterparts. A Lesbian should act and look mannish. But it just wasn't so, either way!

The girl's panties were low cut, like a bikini, made of dainty, see-through black lace. Her stomach was flat, hips wide.

"How about another drink?" Connie was offered.

"Girl, are you beautiful!" came a delighted cry, when Connie stripped. "I didn't realize how beautiful!"

She said, defensively: "I don't know if I should take that as a compliment or a cut!"

"I *mean* it, honey. *How* I mean it!" The voice was husky. "I've seen a lot of naked girls and you're *tops!*"

Her arm brushed Connie's breasts as she started to pour straight Vodka into her glass. The touch was startlingly pleasant, sexually stimulating!

After a few sips on the drinks came a command to dance.

Connie didn't even get a chance to object before she was cushioned against soft breasts. It was a strange, not unpleasant feeling.

Then Connie felt warm hips rubbing against hers.

"You're so soft, Connie," was a soft whisper in her ear. "Very soft and nice. I like soft things. I love to feel a soft body against mine."

Now for the first time Connie felt alarm. But the woman was holding her very tight, just swaying to the music.

The liquor and the sensual actions against her suddenly blended into a strangely erotic combination. At first

115

she equated it as desire for a man, not just raw sexual desire for release.

Then the magic question: "Ever let a woman love you, Connie?"

Then, "I mean, like you were masturbating, except you don't have to do anything but lay back and relax, enjoy caresses and kisses. It can be good. Let me show you." Her tongue played with Connie's earlobe, her hips slipped back and forth again.

"A girl knows about pleasing a woman—differently, of course—but I know where it will feel best...hey why don't we just do it...I'm really turned on!"

Suddenly the idea sounded vaguely appealing. Her body was automatically reacting to the pure physical stimulation of the female flesh.

"Come on, Connie, I'll show you. I'll show you something you wouldn't believe!"

Connie was drunk and she knew it. She felt much like the time that she had first been seduced, not caring, only wanting an orgasm. Her body had always been hot after that first night. The idea of something different, new, was almost exciting in itself.

When they got down on the bed, moist lips covered her breasts with kisses, Connie felt wild desire flush up through her in tingling waves that raced through every nerve. She was clawing the bedcovers, then was moaning and clutching at the woman's back, caressing her and straining up against the hungry kisses. She found it difficult to tell the difference between this woman's lips and those of a man. It simply didn't matter. Other than the fact that this was a wonderfully skilled lover. The pointed tongue played erotic games with her nipples, making Connie gasp in joyous pleasure. A hand slipped under the elastic band of her panties as hungry lips glided down across her stomach. And now she was simply going crazed with desire. She didn't want the other woman to stop touching her, kissing her, devouring her. She wanted to give this lover total freedom to seek out every nerve center with those lovely lips.

Then the woman was going down on her and she was almost wild with the pleasure of it all. Then the dildo, sud-

116

denly entered her body and a sharp thrill raged through her at a sudden invasion she hadn't expected. It wasn't quite like a man, but lasted longer, giving her such a series of climactic pleasures that simply wouldn't stop. There was no ending flutter of orgasm from a man climaxing, but instead a deliciously continuous series of penetrating caresses that didn't stop until she was totally exhausted and...awareness faded out.

CHAPTER NINE

David's voice broke Connie's thoughts away from the past like a knife cutting a think thread.

Guilt flushed over her face as she realized how the erotic memory had charged her body. It was the first time a woman had made love to her. She hated herself for such things.

She looked up at David. She was already partly aroused by her thoughts and now became fully excited by the abrupt nearness of this tall strong, male she had known so intimately for a whole wonderful summer. He was the only man she had ever loved in a real way or desired so totally. What was between them had always been between them. It was nothing but their melding soul blending together.

"What're you girls doing? I walk into the house to find you both in a total blackout."

Pat smiled up at him. "We're just all talked out. I was thinking about Eddie, wondering if he missed us. He'll be coming home in a week. We haven't received any word from him all week."

David laughed. "You can't expect a seven year old boy to be writing letters home."

"Well, at least a 'Hi, Mom and Dad.'" Pat laughed self-consciously. "A picture...phone call. He's so young."

"Out on a farm with all those animals and the other boys to play with. He probably doesn't even miss us."

"That's a horrible thing to say, David!" Pat cried, putting her sewing on the lamp stand beside her.

David looked at Connie.

"What do you think?"

His eyes were half glazed from drink, but there was

118

the hot lust there. Connie wondered if Pat noticed it. Possibly. "I don't blame her, Dave. But...boys will be boys, won't they?"

Her own thoughts were racing with sensual images of David. She could see that at this very moment he was fully aroused.

How long can I take this kind of mental punishment? Connie wondered, annoyed. *I want him so badly I can hardly stand it. And he's hot as hell for me!*

"Well, I guess I'll go out for a ride. It's not too late. Want to join me, you guys?" She included both of them but inwardly meant only David.

"No, enough riding for me for one night," David said. But his eyes, as they met hers, seemed to be longing with desire.

It's funny, Connie thought, as she stood, *how a woman could know her man so well that it was almost as if she were able to hear his thoughts. Even after all these years. Or is it my imagination?*

Was she dreaming or wishing? Connie doubted that. They had meant too much to one another. Their luncheon the day before had offered too many possibilities.

No. David wanted her—and now!

She stood, said: "Well, you stay-at-homes, I'm going out on the town."

"Are you sure you can drive?" David sounded concerned.

"Of course I can. Haven't had *that* much to drink."

"Dear," Pat said in a guarded voice, "why don't you drive Connie. It might be safer."

Connie caught David's eyes then and for a fleeting moment there was little doubt about the open desire burning there. He wanted to go with her; but didn't dare.

"No," he told Pat, "I'm just too pooped."

Connie laughed. "You two. You are cards. You'd think I'd never been out in the world. What do you think I did in Hollywood? There were many times when I had to do the driving. And throw a date into bed—because he was too smashed to even walk straight. Don't worry about me! I'm able to take care of myself."

119

With that she moved to the front hall, then to the outer door.

"Where're you going?" David's voice called.

"Just *out!* For a ride, I guess." A couple of minutes later she was sitting behind the wheel of her '57 Ford, trembling. After starting the car, she gunned it down the street so quickly that the wheels screamed in resistance. Before she knew it, Connie was driving outside town, headed toward Benson City, some twenty miles away. She had to get as much distance between herself and David as possible.

Her mind was whirling from a long series of memories of Hollywood, men's hot, sweaty bodies joining with hers in the lustful games of love and passion, lonely times when only the name of David screamed in her thoughts.

She passed the *Highway Motel* where David had first taken her.

Benson City loomed ahead, glittering in neon signs that flickered on both sides of the road, announcing motels, liquor stores, cocktail lounges.

Connie pulled up in front of a small motel, lined with large green trees that were shadows against the night. She slammed on the brakes, then killed the engine.

There was a liquor store across the street and a bar one block away. A perfect setup for what she had in mind.

Opening her purse, Connie counted three twenty-dollar bills and several singles. Enough to take care of an all-night pleasure trip. She had realized, while driving, that this was the only means of escape open for her.

Connie understood that she felt wild panic. There were only two means of escape from such madness; David or another man—any man.

A moment later she stepped into the office of the motel. Five minutes after that she walked out of the rented. Her bra and panties had been placed in the nightstand, along with most of the money.

The night air was cooling on her face and for a moment she was almost able to feel excited, happy in the knowledge that very soon physical ecstasy would burn away all thoughts. Her whole body took on a new stance, the muscles contracting so that she walked like a sensual animal.

120

The moon bathed softly in the sky, stars twinkled like tiny diamonds flung against the backdrop of velvet. Trees lined the street on either side, and the scent of summer was heavy in the air around her. She felt raw hot tingles wave through every nerve.

As she stepped into the cocktail lounge and discovered that it was half filled with men, a welling excitement moved deep within her. There were only two other women in the place; neither could stand up against her.

Connie found a small table near the center of the room, which gave an excellent view of the men at the bar. Several heads turned in her direction and she stared back, frankly letting them know that she was open to any taker.

Sexually on the make. Brazen, bold. All alone at a small table which invited somebody to join her.

A flush of hotness began to heat her cheeks as the waitress came to the table.

"I'll have a double Martini," Connie ordered, her eyes turned to a tall, sandy-haired young man at the end of the bar who was looking her way. He was broad-shouldered and looked like a real stud.

She smiled and waited.

The man hesitated only long enough to pick up his drink, then stepped over to her, before the waitress had left.

"Can I buy you a drink?" he offered in a friendly, confident voice. There was something about his manner that was commanding and all male. He expected her to take the offered drink without question. His eyes burned down her body, as if stripping off every piece of clothing.

Connie shrugged, feeling wonderfully naked under his stare.

He sat down, said: "My name's Ted."

"Connie." His voice even thrilled her. She *was* hot!

His knee touched hers and the contact was erotically stimulating. Connie felt the desire bursting through her. But they would have to play out the light conversational gambit before it would be possible to leave.

"New in town?" Ted inquired.

"New in town. By myself and nothing to do," Connie announced, deciding to be as direct as possible. "I'm staying

121

at the motel down the street. Just arrived."

"Oh," His left hand reached under the table and touched her leg. That was *his* move to break through the immediate social polite freeze.

Connie winked as his fingers pressed caressingly against the inner curve of her thigh and she squeezed her legs together around them.

He was direct, bold in his move. Connie liked that. The man was good-looking, his face clean cut. It would probably be good with him. She imagined he must have a big erection already building between his legs. The mental image that created was almost funny—and very exciting.

The drink came and Connie saluted with the glass. "Well, Ted, thanks for the drink. I hope you'll let me return the favor."

"Wouldn't think of it."

Connie merely smiled and tried to think of some way to get the two of them out of there once the drink was finished.

Ted asked: "Where do you come from?"

"Hollywood, right now," Connie admitted, watching for his reaction.

Ted's eyebrows went up with surprise. "I'd almost believe you if you claimed to be in the movies. You're certainly beautiful enough."

Connie considered telling the truth, then felt he might be frightened off.

Instead she merely smiled. "Not everybody is in the pictures out there. They do have waitresses, secretaries, a little of everything."

"Ever see any stars?"

"No," she lied. "They don't walk around loose on the streets all the time." Connie finished off her double Martini, as he asked: "Would you like another?"

"Not right now." She shook her head. "This place is terribly noisy, don't you think?"

"For a weekday, yes." His hand left her thigh.

"We could go somewhere else," Connie suggested brightly.

He stood. Without a word the two of them went out-

122

side. Connie nodded in the direction of the motel but moved toward the liquor store across the street.

A short time later they stepped into the small motel room Connie had rented. Ted took the bottle of whiskey he had brought into the bathroom and a moment later returned with two glasses, half filled with liquor.

Connie was sitting on the bed, feeling hot need, as he came down beside her. Neither of them had spoken much since leaving the cocktail lounge.

Now Ted asked, "Staying in town long?"

"No, just the evening—but *all* evening." She took a sip of her drink, feeling suddenly nervous and annoyed.

Everything seemed awkward and Connie didn't want it to be awkward. The liquor, so far, had created little effect on her body.

Ted placed a hand on her thigh. "Mind if I ask you how such an attractive woman like yourself is all alone?"

"Because I *like* it that way!" Connie snapped back. She stared at Ted. "Let's stop being so damned formal!" She bluntly reached between his legs. He was very well developed—hard as hell. "I want that!"

Then Connie stood up and quickly pulled her sweater over her head. A thrill passed through her as Ted gaped up at her naked breasts, his mouth open, tongue licking dry lips. He reached up, fondled one of her breasts, playing with her nipple until it grew hard and tense.

She laughed, lightly slapped his hand away. "Give a girl a chance to undress," she said huskily. "You'll get all you want!"

As she started to slip out of her skirt, Ted stood, pulled off his jacket and opened his shirt. His chest was hairy, like an ape's. She remembered how thrilling it was to rub her breasts against such a chest. Her nipples started to tingle, hardening at the thought.

She watched as he undressed, pleased to discover that his body was hard, muscular. A pleased, low laugh came from deep within her throat at seeing how big and hard he already was.

His eyes swept over her with sudden lust. As he stepped forward, Connie moved back toward the bed. He reached out, pulled her close, one hand covering her right breast, the other finding her curved fanny, squeezing. She thrilled to the curly hairs on his chest where they tickled her erect nipples. Another wave of pleasure passed through her at the nearness of his male body, now even more aroused by the hot embrace. She captured him between her thighs. His lips found hers, greedy, tongue dancing deep into her mouth. Connie responded wildly. Almost uncontrollable need was burning deep.

He felt huge between her squeezing thighs and she twisted teasingly as the kiss broke for breath. He gasped in her ear: "You're wild, lady!"

She laughed, delighted, squeezing her thighs tight together and said: "I'm crazy wild and you better have a lot of energy in that thing...I'm very needy."

Ted lifted her up in his strong arms lips coming in instant contact, open, tongues feasting on one another and then suddenly they were stretched out on the bed and she felt his body deliciously hard in her arms, his lips covering her breasts with voluptuous kisses, moving from one to the other, hotly causing mad pleasure to rip through her. She sobbed, then went suddenly wild in the utter joy of having a man doing such things to her. How every nerve screamed in utter joy.

His hands moved down over her stomach, then caressed quickly across her thighs. Connie tensed, moaned.

She felt sharp mounting excitement, and now could think of nothing else but the need for him. Her own hands reached down and pulled him to her. He moaned with sudden pleasure as she frantically directed him into the confines of her flesh. Then her hands ran over the hard muscles of his back and shoulders and arms, excited by the hardness of him as he moved gently in rhythm with her own body actions. With every passing second the mounting pleasure climbed higher and higher until she was gasping, clawing at his back, straining with every nerve until she couldn't stand it any longer. Connie felt the man strain down like rigid steel, his muscles convulsing in the last moment of his own pleasure.

Neither of them moved for a long time merely lay there, clutching one another tight. Finally he lifted from her and lay down on the bed.

"You were good, love," he announced in a tired, but pleased voice. "Red hot good! You know how to take a man tight and hard!"

Connie laughed, throatily. "You ain't seen nothin' yet!"

With that she turned on her side, started caressing his chest and stomach, pleased by the little rippling muscles that moved under her searching fingers.

"You're really something" he moaned softly.

"I'm turned on, Ted. And when I turn on it takes a real man to do me up pink. I want a lot of loving tonight. Think you can handle it?"

He laughed lightly, as she brazenly reached and explored his groin. "Boy, how lucky can a guy get?"

He touched her shoulder, started to turn.

"No," Connie scolded in mock anger, "let's do it *my* way, this time! Just lay back, big boy, and enjoy yourself."

She slipped closer and now kissed his hairy chest, then her tongue moved along the hard muscles of his stomach. She laughed inwardly. He was going to like the next few minutes, Connie thought, grabbing hold of his thighs. "I'm gonna blow you away!"

"You're wild!" After that he didn't say anything for a long time.

CHAPTER TEN

David sat in his office thinking about the night before. Pat had wanted to make love to him, but he couldn't, not after what had happened with Freda. He would have felt cheap and guilty. He'd claimed to be too tired. For several hours he had lain in bed, thinking about Connie, wondering what she was doing, guessing she might be with a man. The idea angered him. He almost wished he'd taken Freda's offer. At least it would have been an escape from the haunting annoyance of Connie.

Once he almost woke Pat, to make love to her; but fear that he might fail stopped him. It was then that he seriously considered the idea of seducing Freda on their next meeting; just to prove, one way or another, if it was Pat or himself causing his failure.

Now, sitting at his desk, waiting for a phone call from Freda, David wondered if he could ever go through with such a plan. It would be simple enough as far as Freda was concerned. But one part of his mind argued that it would be impossible for him to do it. Yet, he was scared silly he'd take Connie before she left town. It would be cheating on Pat; no less than sleeping with Freda. Yet with a difference.

He was almost desperate to deal with his feelings concerning Connie; to bring them to an end, resolve long held unfinished business with her.

The phone rang; he quickly picked up the receiver. It was Connie.

"Hello, Dave."

An overwhelming thrill raced down his spine. A flush heated his cheeks and suddenly it took a moment to keep from screaming at her. He didn't even know what he wanted

126

to scream. Maybe begging her to go away with him, somewhere, anywhere, so they could be alone to furiously satisfy the longing hurt every time he thought of her, saw her.

"Where are you?" he inquired, wondering if she was okay. She had not returned home by the time he came to work, and they had been somewhat worried.

"In Benson City, at a motel." Her voice sounded intimately inviting, totally unlike the last few days.

"Is everything all right?"

"Wonderful! I'm a little stoned, that's all. My car broke down, and it's in the repair shop. I was just wondering if you could come out and pick me up?"

David immediately realized what she was leading into. "Can't you take a cab?"

"Is *that* what you want, Dave?" Connie sounded disappointed. "I thought maybe you could leave work early and...well, Pat would never have to know."

Here it was; more direct than he might have wished. Connie being drunk explained a lot.

David hesitated, not sure what to say. Every thought screamed for Connie.

"I don't know if I can make it. Tell me where you're staying, I'll call back later."

Connie's voice was thick with annoyance. "You aren't giving me the runaround, are you?"

"No. Just don't know if I'm free this evening. Business, you know." David was sweating; he felt shaky, sick inside.

"Oh. I'm sorry, Dave. Maybe I shouldn't have called and suggested it and—"

"Connie! I'll call you, okay?"

She gave him the number of the motel and then suddenly hung up. David sat there, trembling.

Now all he had to do was leave the office, drive to the motel. In thirty minutes he could be holding Connie, naked, her body soft, yielding, hot against his. So simple.

Frank Nathan stepped into the office at that moment, leaving the question about Connie unanswered. Frank's face was beet-red; hard, cold fury.

"I just talked to Miss Hendricks!" He stepped in front

127

of David's desk. "I don't like what that bitch had to say!"

"Now what's wrong?" David looked up at the man, felt his ulcer grind.

"She claims it is impossible to do business with you. She said you don't bend, aren't reasonable and that you had better come across with an intelligent offer—or she will look elsewhere! I don't know what the hell you did to her last night, but that whore was furious. She didn't mince words, either. What the hell happened?"

"Nothing, except we couldn't agree on the price. But I would guess you know *that* already! I didn't let her push me around." David gazed coldly at Nathan, unflinching. "I gave you her counter-offer this morning."

For a moment the man stood, not speaking, then his shoulders relaxed. It was obviously hard for him to admit David was in the right. "Well, I'll have to say you didn't do anything too out of line...other than annoy Miss Hendricks. But you'll have to come to *some* agreement. She said to have you go over to her hotel this evening, at five. There was no questioning the appointment. It was a command. I accepted for you. She sure is one hard-nose, demanding bitch! Talked up a storm, didn't give me a chance to say more than yes, sir." Nathan shrugged. "It's *your* baby! You ride with it, boy. You don't let her push you around. You make a deal with her this evening. Understood!"

Nathan left the office without another word.

David picked up the phone, dialed the motel where Connie was staying.

* * * * * * *

Connie felt sick inside as she listened to David's voice tell her it was out of the question this night. All day she had been sitting in the motel room thinking about David and herself; and the right she had to live her own life, any way she damned pleased! Something had happened to her the night before; something that had brought out a more basic attitude about life.

Everything she had done in her thirty odd years of life had been centered around a slow self-destruction of hap-

128

piness.

In Hollywood she had learned a bitter truth about life: you either fought dirty or you lost. She was losing— completely. Not only David, but her own grip. Ever since realizing that the three years of marriage to Larry had been a total failure, Connie had been coming to the conclusion that her life had been a failure, too.

She should have married David, years ago! That, maybe, had been the biggest mistake in her life. But, as somebody pointed out to her, one had to reach the mountains in order to understand they weren't as magnificent as imag- ined, and no better than the local ones had been. It wasn't so much that the town she had grown up in was good or bad, nor that Hollywood in itself was bad, simply that one's choices on how to use the tools offered in life could make the difference between happiness and total failure.

This morning, after Ted had left the motel room, Connie had become disgusted at what she had done. Ted gave all a woman could want from a one night stand; but that wasn't what she had really desired, after all. It had merely served to prove that escape was nothing more than running away from herself. For hours she had sat thinking about call- ing David.

When David had finished speaking, Connie said: "Well, I'm staying here, Dave. If you change your mind...I'll be waiting. You understand that?"

"Connie, have a heart."

"Why should I? I want you. You want me. Why should we play games. We're adult creatures. Pat has had you all these years. For the first time in my life, I'm being totally honest with myself and you. When I came back, I didn't know it consciously—but I wanted you, I needed you. And I must have you. I'm at the end of my rope! Believe me. I'm not kidding. Think about it, Dave. Think how easy it would be—for both of us!"

David fell silent, then sighed. "I'll think—that's all!"

The receiver went dead in her hands and Connie turned, lay back on the bed, thought about the night before. It had been sexual, dirty, degrading. A part of her had always felt that way the next morning, after such an orgy. But she

129

was very skillful in submerging such depressive moods, escaping them, or simply getting so drunk that it didn't matter any more.

Something changed. Maybe it was a combination of events Seeing David had shocked a part of her out of the emotionally drugged state which had held her in such a vile grip these last years. The truth, to some extent, had been once she moved to Hollywood to make it in the big city there was no backing down, no returning home with her tail between her legs; she was committed to a life that, in time, eluded her. But desperation and pride had caused Connie to cling desperately to a dying dream, a flawed life-style, frightened to let go, frightened to step back and retrace her moves, life, to center herself.

Now, back home, the only place she had ever been fully successful, had changed her viewpoint. Here she'd been a prom queen in high school, popular, everybody had known her, and she had a wonderful guy who wanted to get married. In Hollywood she was one of an unlimited number of so-called prom queens and Miss County this, and Miss State that. All the beauty queens and kings made it there to seek a place in the heavenly skies of the Movie World! What a life. Sin City, filled with street whores and casting couch tramps selling themselves for illusions that never offered more than a bad scene, a party, a motel room, a quick thrill for some grossed-out middle aged agent, casting director, or producer. These people used wannabees and struggling actors as pleasure toys too stupid to know they didn't have enough talent to do much more than serve as a one-night stand.

Then the real kicker was when one got a part, and could be used by their fellow actors as an object to satisfy deeply scarred egos.

And the real topper: like when she was on tour with a trio, doing one night stands or even a gig lasting a few days or weeks, the loneliness crushed in and the public, the night-club, saloon johns offered up pawing hands and trembling bodies wanting to bed down the celebrity lady on stage. Sucker groupie types who never got past the stage of slipping out at night and cheating on their wives or girl friends, or simply trying to make it with that singin' gal in the sexy

130

oh-so-revealing gown. The customers believed she was looking at them, personally, when singing a love song or flirting wild promises of hot nights together, when usually she didn't even focus on the people in the audience. In fact she couldn't see much in the dimly lighted rooms, nor did she want to. She sang and flirted with faceless shadows that later came up, after the show, attempting to build on their fantasy that she'd been giving them a come-on from the stage. And, sometimes it didn't matter. If the jerk looked promising, she had all too many times, accepted his offer of a cocktail, and later a tail of his cock in a motel room.

And that's just how she thought of it. Meaningless male cocktails. To serve a meaningless, empty hole in her soul, one that never got filled, for she had emptied it of all feeling.

She had simply drowned such things when she left her home to discover Hollywood. She had murdered the Connie that was truly in love with David. The better part of her had died slowly, unaware that it had been so brutally and uncaringly murdered by false ambition, distorted dreams, fantasy madness. The Dream Factory of Hollywood PR had fed into her illusions, and for a while she had held to them. She had believed that if she did what was required, no matter how trite and degrading, somebody would come along to help her, something would happened to elevate failure into instant success. Every star had to struggle, had years of hell before experiencing over-night success. All a person had to do was keep fighting, not give up, and it could happen to them, too.

Sure. Of course. And the cemetery was filled with crushed and destroyed bodies of men and women who never made it beyond the start line.

Some, like her, had managed to survive this far without giving into the destructive impulse. And even success had proved to be a road to depraved death. Happiness wasn't in stardom, but in setting realistic goals and embracing them fully.

David would have been a realistic destination. All she had to do was look at what he had managed to create with her sister. Even with the couple's obvious problems, most of

131

which everybody ended up surviving through, Pat had managed to build a sound life for herself.

One that Connie would rip to shreds if necessary. David had been hers from the beginning. They were destined for one another. Soul mates. Pat had stepped in and grabbed him away. It didn't matter that Connie had walked out on a wonderful relationship and dumped him. That was something a man could forgive the woman of his life. And nobody in this Small Town, U.S.A could compete against her, not in the end. If nothing else, Connie had learned how to play dirty, if necessary, and how important winning could be, and how losers deserved to suffer defeat if they didn't fight for keeps.

Pat had had her chance and she could fight her own battles to keep David in line. If that was possible, now.

But Connie knew her man. And she had seen the hunger in his eyes, felt the tension the instant they had embraced so innocently the other day. More, she knew him as totally as if he were merged into her very soul. He was unhappy. Why, they hadn't gotten around to share those details. But it was time to help him make some life-course corrections.

If she wanted her man, she would have to fight for him. It was that simple.

Anything else would be another defeat. And Connie couldn't face that.

Not now. And not knowing how deeply David still hungered for her. The fact was the he'd always been hers; and he had been waiting here all these years, just treading water until she returned. Well. Now she was back. And he could have what he always wanted.

Yes, she told herself, *I love him. I always did. So don't kid yourself, Connie. You kept away from this town all those years, because you knew he was here for the taking— and at the time it didn't seem right to come back and claim your man, who had build a life with....*

She ripped that thought away. Avoiding it like a deadly poison.

Life without David had become a nightmare. A big mistake. She didn't want to go back to the world that had

132

swallowed down eleven years, and made her into something alien from the young girl who had left her hometown.

She didn't like herself that way. She didn't like the kind of whoring bitchy slut she became!

Connie reached down to the floor, picked up the half empty bottle of gin she had purchased several hours before.

Life's hell; all of it, she thought, taking a swallow of gin. She felt as if she were at a dead end. There were only a few directions left to go. Male pricks dicking her; or real love. Survival! David.

David was all that was left worth fighting for.

She sat up in bed, sipped more gin. For a few years, and for the last few days, especially, Connie had managed to fool herself into believing there was another way to survive than mere self-interest! She had to win, no matter who got hurt in the process.

Pat was always in the way, and as a baby had grabbed young love from their parents, stepped into Connie's private world, shattered the total, single-minded love that had been only hers, in the beginning. Now, again, it was *Pat* who had taken the love away—claimed the only man Connie had ever really loved.

"Damn it all!" Connie cursed at the walls, determination smothering all sense of guilt. "Damn you Pat, you're the only thing that's kept me from Dave, just because you're my sister. To hell with you! And what the hell did you ever do to earn such loyalty? Screw you! If you had been another woman I'd taken David long before now. But...now he'll be mine! All mine!"

She would take David from Pat—get him back in her arms, *forever!*

* * * * * * *

David had a couple of Scotches at the cocktail bar across the street from where he worked, then drove out to the Highland Hotel; hardly feeling the drinks. His ulcer burned, but the physical annoyance was little compared to his mental turmoil about Connie and Freda. Connie's open offer would be easy to take; too easy! Her surprising change of attitude

133

actually frightened him. Would it be possible to control her; or himself?

A sense of uneasiness disturbed David as he drove the car in the parking lot of the Highland Hotel. The surrounding countryside was quiet, an air of peacefulness rested on the land around him. So much green, rich and beautiful; trees spotting the distant hills. All his life he had spent in this country; it was home to him in so many ways. As a young teenage boy he had roamed these very hills, long before the hotel was built. Played Tarzan, right out of the movies, then later out of the books by Edgar Rice Burroughs. As a child he'd wanted to travel to Africa, and then other romantic seeming places. Years had changed his dreams of adventures in foreign lands to desires of love and marriage. But those dreams were shattering. Now in his mid-thirties he was on the edge of illicit sex.

David put out his cigarette and then left the car, starting for the hotel. He didn't want to think about Connie.

The hotel desk clerk told him that Miss Hendricks was in her room.

When he knocked on Freda's door he had to wait some time before she answered. When the door opened, he heard the sound of a shower going.

She stood before him with a blue bathrobe pulled tightly around her voluptuous body. Obviously there could be nothing under the robe but her naked flesh.

David found himself tense in almost alarm, then a warm glow tingling down his spice.

All his mind could think of was that the woman was stark naked under that robe and her body was boldly outlined against the terry-clothe. And, most unnerving was how the top was hardly modestly clutched shut, but carelessly held as if grabbed quickly. The sight of one lush breast was teasingly revealed almost to the nipple. It couldn't have been more perfectly framed if she'd calculated it that way for some photo-shoot in a men's magazine.

"I'm sorry, David," she murmured softly, not sounding in the least bit sorry, "but I was late getting back, and was just showering. Do you mind if I finish?"

He wondered if she had calculated everything, and if

134

this wasn't a seductive setup.

She quickly closed the door behind him. "Make yourself at home. There's some of the Scotch you like on the night stand. Help yourself. I'll be out in a few minutes."

With that, she turned and went into the bathroom, closing the door behind her.

David made his way to the night stand. Two glasses, a bucket of ice and a small silver pitcher of cream stood beside an unopened bottle of Scotch. The same expensive brand as the night before.

In the background, as he opened the bottle, he heard the sound of light humming coming from the bathroom, accompanied by the shower. It was an inviting and intimate combination; and no doubt well-planned to be that way. A skillfully designed seductive trap!

Suddenly he felt shaken, trembling. If she walked out of that bathroom in the nude it would be impossible to deny the fulfillment of any demand she might made of his body. She would seduce him without even trying.

Sipping the Scotch, David tried to figure Freda Hendricks. She certainly was not the kind of woman who needed to get kicks by throwing herself at any business contact who came along. She was lovely enough to have her pick of lovers.

David finished off his drink, then refilled the glass. There was a chair sitting next to the huge bay-windows, and he sat down, staring out at the rolling hills, for a moment thinking about his childhood, when all the problems in the world centered on what might be over the next hill. Life, David realized, was an endless repetition of that same questing; but the hills became different, the destinations harder to reach, more rewarding.

The shower stopped, and David strained to hear Freda's movement in the bathroom. Part of him hoped she would come out stark naked and present him with no option but to take her. A flush touched his cheeks at the thought that she might do just that. It could be a natural trick for her to play.

He was half finished with the Scotch and cream when the bathroom door opened. She had the blue robe pulled

135

tightly around her body. He could see the points of her nipples press against the cloth. The sight was far too effective. In fact more effect than if she wasn't wearing the robe. It teased without being demanding, it flaunted that she knew just how to entrap a man's raw needs and set them on fire. It alerted him that she was not stupid enough to be crude, not some slut on the make, but a very sharp lady doing whatever was necessary to win a game of her own making. And at that moment it was obviously being seductive without blatantly throwing herself at him.

"I'm sorry to keep you waiting. How's the Scotch?"

"Fine."

She moved across the room like a jungle cat, her hips undulating from side to side, her breasts swaying slightly against the robe, the top open just enough to reveal the valley between. "I should change into something more presentable. But...quite frankly, right now I need a drink. I'm really exhausted. I hope you don't mind. I had a hard day, and to be honest I find this much more comfortable. You don't mind, do you?"

Christ, she's all but shoving herself at him, without doing it in so many words.

She paused a couple of feet away, staring down like a demon lover, tempting men to their passionate doom. Red marked her full lips, her eyes were lined, shadowed in blue. The long tapered calves of her legs showed below the bottom of the robe. She gave the appearance of a sophisticated woman of the world, used to presenting herself to endless lovers. And not in the least embarrassed about it.

"Not more than it would bother any man, I suppose," he managed in an effort to appear quite calm and at ease. But she could see just how aroused he was.

"Now, how nice, sometimes I wonder if you really notice." She went to the night stand and helped herself to a stiff drink of Scotch, then tipped the glass to her wide lips.

She studied him for a full couple of minutes, saying nothing, yet her eyes took in every detail, lingering now and then, as if mentally caressing him. Yet the expression in her eyes revealed nothing. Finally she nodded, as if to herself, then looked directly into his eyes.

136

After taking a large swallow of the liquor, she said in a determined voice: "You know, David, the other night was harder on me than I thought it would be."

David's mind screamed in protest. The shift of mood and attitude was so startling that all he could do was sit there desperately attempting to keep control of a situation that she literally was controlling. And she wasn't going to be subtle about it any more.

"I'm sorry," he managed, after taking a swallow of his own drink. Her words had been filled with real emotion and instantly put him on the defensive.

Freda sat on the bed, and the robe gathered up enough to slip above her knees, revealing the naked smoothness of one soft thigh. It was a calculated move to excite any male. She didn't do anything to cover herself up.

Freda laughed lightly.

"What's so funny?"

"You should see yourself. I could almost read your thoughts."

"Don't, please!" He couldn't get his eyes off her.

"Oh, but I only think it's right. You're wondering exactly how far I'll go...how much teasing. Am I being a calculating, seductive lady, or just open and honest and totally at ease with myself. Am I trying to seduce you? Or is this just happening by happenstance, accident? Isn't that right?"

Then before letting him answer, she continued:

"I think I'll let you suffer for a while. I don't mind admitting many thoughts are tempting me, right now. You are one hell of an attractive male, and I did give a lot of thought to you last night. I mean—*you,* not the business. A woman like me sees things far more clearly than a man in your position. You think about your wife and your child and reputation. I have no reputation to worry about. I'm single. Sex is so simple a thing, really. Not complicated at all. A man and woman want to climb in bed with each other—and that's all there is to it. They get a few thrills. Some shared laughs; enjoy one another. I really don't see why married men make so much of it. Maybe because they get confused by their wives. Married women never admit to themselves that sex without love can be just as physically pleasing—that

137

it isn't necessary to be emotionally involved. Most men understand that, because they approach sex in a different way. Men know they can enter into a sexual relationship with other women without hindering their love for the wife back home."

She winked. "Now tell me, honestly.... Don't you agree?"

David was trying to follow her reasoning, attempting to see a loophole in it, but at the moment she sounded too logical.

"I guess you could look at it that way," David admitted, carefully, hoping to avoid any agreement that would automatically lead into a sex-scene.

She shrugged. "Well, I've put my cards on the table, David, I guess you know that."

"I know it," he admitted, huskily, avoiding her eyes.

Freda stood, and the robe parted slightly, enough to show the parting of her breasts. David felt an unwanted reaction. She glided to him.

"I hope you don't think I'm some sort of kook, but I never believe in panting around the bush, so to speak. I come right out and say what I think; and what I want." She stepped closer, her robe opening as she moved. Now he could see the pink nipple of her left breast peek out around the fold of blue cloth.

"Don't you really think we should get down to business?" David suggested, trying to *sound* business-like.

"Is that what you want?" Freda asked, not attempting to hide her surprise. She stood before him, the robe almost completely open; she was totally naked underneath.

David felt his throat go dry, he couldn't keep his eyes off that body. His nerves screamed to stand, take her fast, hard, cruelly. It was what she deserved.

Then the image of Pat came in front of her.

"Miss Hendricks, I think it's best we take care of the business, *now!* I'm not about to be seduced by your little frontal attack. I *do* believe it fair to warn you that even if I were to make love to you, it wouldn't make one difference as to the offer on the contract."

She retreated two steps as if slapped. Her face took

138

on a hard, nasty expression, the lips curled, the eyes narrowed with abrupt emotion.

David mentally sighed out his relief. It was over. His body ached with desire, which was unbearable. It was then he knew what he would do about Connie.

Freda said in a cold voice: "Well, Mr. Carter, I must admit, you are a cut different from other men."

"Don't push your luck, too far," David warned. "I have an offer here which is *rock* bottom! I can't cut lower; and that's it! The papers are all in order. You can simply call me at the office when you have decided to either take or leave it."

Freda reached out her right hand, palm up, her face still ashen, stubborn; hard as steel. "Well, we'll see if it's *rock bottom* or not."

David opened his briefcase, finding it hard to keep from trembling. Finally he pulled out a folder and handed it to her.

She snapped the folder open, glanced over the figures. Shaking her head, she said: "I'm sorry. I don't think we can do business at all. The prices quoted here are way out of line." She looked up into his eyes; for a moment a softness revealed itself. "But...it will be necessary to present them to the company, with my recommendation to turn them down!"

"I'm sorry, Miss Hendricks, but we can't and won't go any lower. We aren't in the business to lose money. You *do* understand?" He felt sick inside; the grind of his ulcer felt like a painful knife turning there. Everything was going down the drain, simply because he had not been willing to climb into bed with Freda. It seemed ridiculous, but that seemed to be the facts. Maybe if he had given Freda what she wanted, it might have been possible to convince her to deliver a recommendation in his favor. But he wasn't about to prostitute himself for any job. So, out went the promotion.

David felt bitterness eat hungrily at him as he turned to leave.

"I wish things had turned out better," he said in parting.

Freda shrugged. "Don't think it's been a pleasure—for it hasn't! But I won't hold that against you. Business is

139

business. And if you believe it or not, the fact that you didn't screw me has nothing to do with the fact that I think your offer is a bunch of crap!"

David tried to smile, but he had to get away from her. "I'm sorry you feel that way about it."

"Think *nothing* of it. It's pure business. And, anyway, I don't have the final word. To be truthful, David, I sorta like you, even if you are screwing loyal to your wife. Maybe *because* of that!"

Then suddenly her mood changed like rapid-fire. She smiled, and with one quick motion dropped her robe away, letting it fall to the floor.

Stunned, David stood, frozen, as she stepped boldly forward, slipped her arms around his neck, thrust her hips at his, her thigh finding a natural place between his legs, pressing a very painful erection straining tightly against confining slacks.

"Not even a screwing loyal husband can turn down this kind of offer!" she murmured, a pleased expression on her lips. Her thigh wiggled back and forth. "You have a big hard for me, David, why don't we stop playing all these cute little games and screw ourselves silly?"

David felt hot, so hot it was impossible to stand it, then her lips were covering his neck and cheeks with voluptuous hot tongue kisses. He was aware of her wiggling against his stiff erection, the flush nakedness of her breasts cushioned to his chest. Her whole body was all but raping him, right through the clothing.

When her lips met his, open, almost sucking, he couldn't control the impulse to cooperate. They were suddenly tongue kissing and his hands were all over her back, into the swells of her fanny, squeezing, fondling. Finally she broke the kiss, stepped back, reached boldly between his legs, fingers making a quick, erotic exploration, then teasingly dropping to her side.

"Get those damned clothes off!"

He backed away, scared silly that it would now be impossible to stop things.

She mocked him with a grin. "I know a lot about you, David. I know something about your Connie Lewis, too. And

140

the reports are, the two of you are screwing-mad about each other. Really stuck it to her that summer, didn't you? Well, why don't we just try each other on for size. I'm safer than that sister-in-law of yours. I won't kiss and tell. I won't complicate matters; *any!* Maybe afterwards we will understand each other better. There's nothing better than a hot fuck between man and woman to build understanding...I might even be willing to be a little easier on you...I might even consider your offer a bit more seriously. All you have to do is give in. What's wrong? Nobody will know. Just the two of us."

She stepped back, moving to the bed, as if drawing him toward the temptation of her passion trap.

Somehow David managed: "What the hell kind of female are you?"

"I'm a hot female. I'm hot all over, David. I've been known to do some pretty wild things, just because I needed it, good and hard, right between my legs. I'm sick hot, right now. Come on, David, you want me. I can see that big cock between your legs just throbbing to get in me. You want me just like I want you. Pure, animal, lusting sex. It is so damned easy. What's wrong, haven't you ever fucked a real woman before?

"Sure, I know men like to be talked to that way, so don't start getting prudish with me. I know you like hearing a woman talk real dirty, and I know all the screwing good words. Come on, love I'll screw you until there's nothing left. I'll show you such a great, orgiastic time you'll think your Connie and even your wife are nothing compared to—"

It was that which gave David the strength. Without a word he turned, got out of there fast, because suddenly he felt an urge to walk over to Freda and violently rape her to silence. She was a widely sexual animal, that deserved to be exhaustively taken by some jolly red giant with a huge pointed tail.

He was shaking all the way to his car, not able to believe what had happened.

Her body, her words, actions, made a man willing to screw the wall in desperation!

* * * * * * *

Freda sank down on the bed, shocked. She'd done everything within her power to bluntly drive David beyond the point of no return. She'd never been that way with a man before; not with a business contact.

Suddenly she wondered about her own motives. Ever since getting the report on David from the detective, ever since meeting him in the flesh, she'd had a frantic desire to possess this man, in total. And all at once, Freda realized it must have been for better reasons than merely business; or pure sex. What, maybe she'd never know. But something about David Carter drove her sexual juices mad.

Maybe because she couldn't have him.

Freda considered that, still stunned, numbed aware that she had met a man who would not—under any circumstances—be seduced by her.

Sick, partly because of the refusal, partly because of the way she'd acted, Freda lay back on the bed, looking up at the ceiling, aware that it would be a long time before she'd get over being so bluntly turned down.

Why was it so important? Because he was handsome, desirable; or because he simply was a loyal husband, not about to be sucked into some erotic trap?

God, she thought, ill inside, *what made men like David Carter tick? He's the first...the very first to turn me down!*

Then sitting up, she cursed: "The dirty bastard! Son-of-a-bitch! What makes him so holy different? To *hell* with him!"

With that, Freda got dressed, decided she might as well go down to the cocktail lounge and pick herself up a loving-man, who would brighten her sexual urges to high pitch; something *free;* someone who would want little old Freda for herself. Then things would look better!

Maybe.

142

CHAPTER ELEVEN

David was a little tipsy as he drove the car along the highway. He kept telling himself that what was going to happen was unavoidable. Yet the panic that assailed his emotions the moment he stepped outside of Freda's hotel room, knowing exactly where he was going, still felt sharp.

Connie was waiting! She didn't care if he got a raise; it wouldn't bother her that he probably would never get a chance to move up or better his position in the firm as long as Frank Nathan was office manager. He'd screwed up the contract because he couldn't screw Freda.

Bitterly, he admitted, his morality was crushingly different from Freda's!

David's foot lifted from the gas pedal. For a moment he almost stopped the car, turned around. Then he reasoned that going to Connie didn't necessarily mean he would sleep with her. She did need a ride back home—at least he should convince her to return even if her car really wasn't ready.

By the time David spotted the motel at which Connie had said she was staying, he was convinced that nothing could possibly happen. Regardless of the fact they both desired each other. They had to consider Pat.

He easily found her room, which was at the far end of the motel. A large oak tree grew outside, a gravel walkway ran along the building, lined with rose bushes. It was a romantic place for a rendezvous. A romantic rendezvous designed for two lovers.

David didn't hesitate as he stepped up to the door. Knocking, he waited, outwardly relaxed, and was almost able to convince himself that everything was going to be okay.

The door opened and Connie leaned against the frame, dressed in a sweater and skirt. She was holding a glass filled with clear liquid in her right hand. Her lips pursed; as if blowing him a kiss.

"Come on in, honey," she breathed out sexily, her breasts expanding against the tight-fitting sweater.

David gaped at Connie, amazed by the change that had overcome her. She was obviously drunk; and far from reserved. She looked wantonly up at him through narrowed lids, took a drag of her cigarette and blew smoke in his face.

"How long are you going to stand out there in the cold of night. Certainly you aren't afraid to enter the chambers of this passionate female?"

She laughed and there was something challenging to it. "Come on, Dave, don't be a bloody fool!"

She grabbed hold of his arm, half dragged him into the room, kicked the door shut with her foot and leaned back against it, posed so that her hips and breasts were thrust at just the right angle to show themselves off most provocatively.

"Come on, Connie, let's go home," David suggested in a far flatter tone than he had expected

"My, my, aren't you the cool one. You actually sound angry at your Connie." She stared directly into his eyes, added seriously: "You *know* that's true! I've always been yours. I'm yours now, Dave. And I'm claiming you for my own."

David's legs trembled, his throat went dry. It was all too much. Illogical as it seemed, everything was quite logical. Never before in his married life had he been thrown into two such remarkable situations with such outstandingly desirable women. But it all fit into a pattern from which he couldn't escape. First Connie coming back into his life; then the dealings with Freda Hendricks that would have easily been slid through—but for Connie.

It was always Connie!

It always had been.

And here they were in a motel room, alone.

Pat would think he was with Freda Hendricks, going over contracts. They could spend the whole evening to-

144

gether; Pat might never guess.

But then what?

He wanted to say they were both leaving right now; but couldn't move. He merely stood there in the middle of the room, looking at Connie. Wanting her. He realized she wasn't wearing any bra, and felt surprised at the youthful firmness of her breasts as they strained against the pink sweater.

He remembered what it had been like with Connie in similar motel rooms. His body reacted immediately at the memory.

Finally he said: "I don't know what you have in mind, Connie, but do both of us a favor and forget it!"

Connie merely shook her head from side to side. "No, Dave. Not *this* time! I have my rights."

"You gave them up, long ago."

"I put them off. But I'm turning back the clock, Dave. I'm taking what's mine. You're mine, you always have been, you always will be. You know that, I know it. Why you married Pat...well, I guess one of the Hollywood head-doctors could give you a nice little pat answer to *that!* I won't bother. It's obvious to both of us. So why fool around? I'm here, you're here. If you didn't want me just as badly as I wanted you, you wouldn't have come. Admit it to yourself. We've been playing a child's game too long! We've been lying to ourselves, trying to find children's explanations for adult problems. We live only once. You can't throw your life away because of a few failed bombs that were dropped in the past. You have the present and future to live! I realized that last night—and it took me some time to admit it to myself. We live once! Make the most of it, to hell with past mistakes. I want you like I want life, Dave. I don't believe in losing you just because somebody else might get hurt. What about us? Life's cruel, Dave. That's the way it is. Neither of us made it that way. It happened. I'm sorry for Pat. That's all I care to say on the subject."

David's head was spinning, his body firing with hot desire, his nerves screaming to have an end to all this physical and mental torment.

"I need a drink," he rasped.

145

"Sure, Dave. Have a drink! Have a whole goddamn bottle if that's what it takes to face the truth. But face life. Face yourself. Be honest for a change. Ever since I returned you've been panting to make love to me. Why deny yourself what's yours to take; if you still have the guts to claim it. Grab life—whatever you can get of it. Live, before it's too late. We're not getting any younger; and there's a lot of years to make up for."

She nodded to the bottle of gin on the table to David's right.

"Connie, we can't let this get out of hand," David said, already afraid that he had weakened beyond the point of resistance. This was what he had been wanting ever since seeing Connie that first day at the house. She was his. All he needed to do was reach out and take her into his arms.

The raw gin burned his throat like fire. Then gentle soothing tendrils worked through his body, momentarily taking away all sense of argument. He felt sensual in a way that overpowered reason. His mind rode on that level as he faced Connie.

She was perversely young for her age, looked not over twenty-five; and a healthy, youthful twenty-five, at that! Her large eyes had the outward surface appearance of innocence; but there was a warmth of hot smoldering maturity in their depths that revealed itself lustfully when she looked at him. Her red lips, full, the lower one pouting out just slightly, gave a mature baby-doll suggestion to that even high cheek-boned face. Her wide forehead was half covered by loose blonde bangs, the face itself framed in long silken flowing hair. That body was excitingly voluptuous, the breasts high, well-formed, self-supporting, dotted by pert points, which showed boldly against the sweater; the waist narrowed, then hips flared out and down into what David remembered as being a remarkable pair of firm exciting thighs. Her stomach looked as flat as it had been years ago. She had kept her youth; how, was a remarkable wonder of nature.

His eyes once again swept along her form, then paused at the well turned ankle, slender, tapering up to curving calves. Connie's feet, like her hands, were proportioned

146

to her body, but gave the appearance of being very delicate. He noticed for the first time that she was barefooted, the nails painted blood-red.

"See, Dave, what I mean?" Connie told him, after he had stared at her for some time, "you can't get your eyes off me."

"Curse you, Connie! Why can't you leave me alone? Why don't you go back where you came from?" David cried, fighting the hot desire now taking control of his very soul.

"I *am* home, David. I couldn't keep away. All these years I've wanted you. All the time I was with other men I knew they couldn't compare to you. We were something special—it just took time for me to realize *how* special. You see it, too, Dave. Don't try to deny it. Your eyes are caressing me like your lips and hands and body want to."

Again David fought against the raw desire attacking him. He tried to turn away, to look at anything other than Connie, but it was impossible. He wanted her more than anything in the world; he had never stopped wanting her. She was like a wild vortex, sucking in around him and drawing him deeper and deeper into its powerful depths.

"We can't do this to Pat," he finally gulped out, frantic.

"We can't do anything else, for ourselves, and you know it, Dave." Her voice was so firm; sure of itself. And the words wrapped themselves around him like caressing waves, stroking the nerves with fiery need. He was dizzy from the total effect of her; hungry to the point of hopelessness. He could no more walk away from this moment, this desire, and this longing need than he could stop breathing.

He felt suddenly ill, deep inside. The conflicting emotions were draining all strength, thought, and ability to reason.

Without a word, David turned, rushed to the bathroom, slammed the door behind him; locked it in panic, as if this would lock out the driving insistent need.

Leaning against the wall, David attempted to control the trembling of his muscles. He was shivering as if in some icy room, yet hot sweat covered his forehead in tiny little beads.

147

Everything that had happened in the last few days flashed through his mind. Then he thought of Pat; remembered how tender and understanding she had been the other night when he failed her. She was a good woman, a good wife and mother. No man could ask for a more wonderful woman with whom to share his life.

Then her words returned to him. She had said it didn't matter if he failed her; that this was far better than sleeping with another woman.

All at once David felt the strength return, determination ran like steel into his nerves. He simply couldn't do it to Pat.

David turned and faced the door. It would be simply a direct *no* to Connie; and he'd leave, go home. Maybe he would even let Pat know the truth. The fact that it was Connie, and he hadn't slept with her, would settle the matter. Pat would agree it was best that Connie left, under the circumstances. Maybe it would strain their relations for a time, but David doubted that, since Pat would know he loved her so completely that even when temptation came, his love was too strong to allow anything to happen that might bring her pain. No, Pat would understand.

David opened the door, stepped out of the bathroom, and then stopped short.

The years slashed away and there was no Pat in his world—for she was something that would cross his life in the future, several years in the future, when he finished college, got a job—after Connie had left for Hollywood. In that instant nothing existed but Connie and himself in a motel room. Time had turned back on itself. Buckled.

Connie lay stretched out under the covers, looking up at him, her eyes promising passion and love, tenderness and affection, a joyful outlet for the wild hungers deep within him. Just like all their times together.

Time frosted over, set, froze, and he was a young man, sharing a motel room with the woman he loved and wanted to marry.

The illusion was more than a mental trick or rationalization—it was real in a sense that all else seemed merely a dream, nothing more.

148

Without a word, David moved to the bed, sat beside Connie, then leaned down, touched her lips with a tender kiss.

Her arms came gently around his neck. Her lips parted eagerly to his kiss and he greedily explored the depths of her mouth, thrilling to the teasing pressure of her tongue and teeth.

"Oh, Connie, Connie, Connie," he moaned a moment later, as his lips touched her throat.

"Connie, oh, God, I love you!"

She purred contentedly, then gently pulled away the blanket from between them. Like she'd done so many times in the past.

Her breasts lay like ovals of soft, yielding flesh, held up by their own natural firmness. The nipples, pink like rosy flowers, topped their peaks, tensely awaiting a lover's kiss.

He slipped the blanket away from her hips and legs until her whole body was exposed to him, ready for the caresses that would fire it up toward the mountain of ecstasy. Her lips merely smiled up at him as he leaned over and kissed each breast, letting his tongue worship around the nipples as they quickly hardened.

Then he stood, started undressing, all the time his eyes taking in the beautiful shape of her body, remembering what it was like to fully possess her.

She moistened her lips with the point of a delicate tongue as he slipped out of his pants, her eyes feasted on his own firmly kept body, openly pleased by what she saw.

David moved to her; and she slipped to one side, to give him room.

Then her arms reached out, drew his body close. She trembled as their lips met in the first kiss of love-play that would lead to all the pleasures of the body, all the ecstasy of love.

For this was love of a special kind, something which had never simmered out, had always been there, lingering in the background of their lives, beings, and souls. This was a moment that had to be lived, experienced, rediscover.

David's hand cupped her breasts, aware of the hardness of a nipple against his palm. Then he caressed down

149

over her stomach, across her hips. She writhed at the intimate touch, and captured his hand between smooth hot thighs, twisting slightly back and forth as their tongues danced in and out, building the rhythm of desire to a quick peak.

He felt her hands search over him, until they discovered the harsh painful erection, stiffly alert, burning passionately for her like a fiery rod desperately needing to be enveloped within her embrace..

He covered her face with kisses, caressed her body with frantic hands, bringing her need up to meet his own, fondling breasts with loving care. He was totally surrendering to the magic of this woman, this wonderful, sensational female, this goddess whom he had never stopped loving, wanting, needing. His whole being throbbed with the longing for her. But he wanted it to last, wanted to know the total beauty of making love to her. His lips found her breasts, circled around the full molded forms, teasing their rosy peaks until she was clawing at him, writhing with her hot desire, begging with every action for the final plunge that would unite them in the long moments of ultimate pleasure.

Her hands found his hips, then eagerly discovered the full length of his erection, her lips murmured something that was more moan of joy than words.

She now possessed him. And her touches, caresses lingered softly, then passionately, then so hungrily intense that it was like being devoured in a rage of mad flames.

Her fingers were dragging him toward the very center of her being. Her hands then gripped his hips and he surged deep within the center of her, as legs twisted tightly about him. He felt her surge slowly around his throbbing hard, lovingly enveloping it deeper and deeper within a velvet embrace. They were both sobbing in the joy of the voluptuous sensations of this first penetration. Then slowly he lifted, then plunged, out of his mind with the pleasure of her body encasing him so eagerly. Then he suddenly tensed, screamed like a wounded animal, losing control of life, trembling against the ecstasy that burst through him. Then she was moving, still holding him as part of her, driving strength back into him, surging renewed desire into life. And with every insistent urging of her hips, David felt the strength, the need create new control until he was joining in her motions, feeling himself going more and more wild with the pleasure being forced into being. Then suddenly Connie screamed, her whole body arched, strained up against his, her mouth parted in gasping, anguished ecstasy.

His own body released itself in her, driving him into a world of pure physical sensations. Nothing else existed.

David drifted back to awareness, his mind flitting over the last ten years, to the present, as if in some perverted time machine skimming into that future and into the real now.

Then the flight was stopped short, reversed, as a gentle hand touched his chest, circled down over his body, searched along his legs, between them, only to reach up to his face as lips covered his. He felt the soft yielding touch of a supple breast cushion against his arm and chest. A feminine hand caressed over him like soft velvet, drawing the exhaustion from his body and replacing it with a slow growing need.

Her fingers became hot fire running over him, flitting away, teasing, and driving him to a new level of madness.

He found Connie's shoulders, pulling her closer. Her body shifted and he felt soft weight slide onto him. She was so much lighter than he would have imagined, so silken soft and warm.

David tried to think, but her tongue was dipping deep past his teeth. She continued to move against him; voluptuously thrilling, her legs caressing his, her hands tensed on his shoulders.

Then her body was controlling his, controlling the love-making, bringing remarkable response when he would have thought it impossible. He felt wave upon wave of pleasure surge through his nerves with every rhythmic move she made. He couldn't think any more. There was only her body, her thrilling and exciting actions driving him up towards a new peak of ecstasy. Suddenly he couldn't take any more. He felt himself flying over the peak. Screaming at himself for not being able to wait, hating his body for not controlling the convulsive response, he felt shameful release.

Connie moaned, more in pleasure than anything else, then lifted from him.

"Dave," she murmured softly, caressing his name with love. Her hand touched his face. "Dave...come..."

He opened his eyes, startled. For a moment he didn't remember what had happened.

"Now, don't fall asleep on me," Connie teased. "We haven't begun—not even begun."

She reached for him, took his hand, urged him up from the bed.

"Have a heart, Connie," he laughed, surprised by her brazen attitude, her casual acceptance of his sudden lack of control that must have left her needing, wanting.

Connie laughed as he stood, then pulled herself into his arms, their bodies flush against one another. "You're great, Dave...wonderful!"

David moaned. "You can say that after what just happened?

Her tongue worried his ear and neck. "Silly man...you just got a little over-excited, that's all. That's what a woman likes; a man who is so excited by her that he can't control himself. Come with me, lover, and I'll show you a few tricks you probably never thought of!"

Connie led him into the bathroom, then turned on the shower.

"What you doing?"

"We're going to take a bath, sexy."

"Are you kidding?"

"Together, in there!" She pulled aside the shower door.

"Don't you think that's a little small?"

She caressed his shoulder, kneading the muscle. "In there, muscles. In there, together, love, my lover, oh, lovely Dave! Don't tell me you never took a shower with a woman before."

"Now, you don't want the answer to that," David teased, getting into the light mood she had so skillfully developed.

Connie tried the water with her fingers. "Come on in, big boy—and let's make love. Just love each other...."

152

David knew she was kidding about the last part, but he slipped into the shower next to her, cramped against her wet body, washed by the hard flow of the warm water.

She slipped her arms around his waist, drawing close. Her hips slid back and forth against him, then they kissed, passionately demanding, the wine of her creating a new surge of excitement.

The dampness of her body as it pressed against his was exciting in a new wild way. Her breasts clung to his chest as if lightly glued there.

Connie giggled as she slid her kiss along his cheek. "See, love, you can't give up too soon."

Her thighs parted, closed about his suddenly stiff shaft, thrillingly.

"Already my lover-man is wanting me," she teased, delighted, twisting back and forth.

All of a sudden uncontrollable excitement captured David. All he could think of was joining her body!

Connie's form moved, her hands grabbed his hard, then pulled him close. After that there was no questioning the possibility that their two forms could join in the dance of passion. He was already submerged within the moist depths of her.

Almost immediately Connie was gasping in hot gulps of air, her mouth wide, her eyes closed tight as racking sounds uttered from deep within her throat. All the time her hands gripped his hips, hammered a rhythm, controlling the movements. Then she trembled convulsively, and her hands fell limp to her side.

He found himself still fired by her embrace, knowing that they hadn't even started. The long years of wanting her, of dreaming about that long summer love they had shared, of desperately needing to recapture what they'd had in their youth together now demanded realization. They could not stop until the hunger had subsided, until they had sated their mutual need. Assuming it could never be satisfied.

"Oh, love, love, you're good," she moaned. Then when he didn't even stop, she cried, "Oh, Dave, Dave, you're driving me...crazy—*crazy!*" She grabbed at him, moaning, thrashing from side to side, then uncontrolled happy laughter burst from her lips. "Dave...Dave...it's... good...*too good*"

Then he was laughing too, out of his mind with joy, unable to stop the delicious movements that kept mounting pleasure jumping over his nerves.

It was insane, fantastic, too much to stand! Then both of them all at once froze in time and ecstasy. A long, lingering moment, an instant, an eternity all spread out between them, through them, around their very beings, then slowly closed, embrace, then in one slow flash faded.

After that they were exhausted, their bodies totally spent. Like moving dead, they washed, then out of the shower, dried one another.

"Want a cigarette?" Connie offered, as they returned to the room.

"And a drink," David laughed, his throat dry. He looked at Connie and remembered the peaks of pleasure that had repeated more than twice within her body.

"A drink and a cigarette. Share one of each with you," Connie suggested, opening her purse and drawing out a pack of cigarettes.

"You are so beautiful, Connie," David announced, pouring the gin into the glass. "Wonderful!"

"I think you're the *best*, Dave—the best there is!" She flopped down onto the bed, then patted the space beside her.

They lay next to one another, hips just lightly touching, sharing the cigarette and gin. It was intimate and pleasant. She kissed his cheek, then patted his thigh. "You've gotten better, Dave. Really better. You know tricks I don't remember enjoying with you before."

David tensed at the statement. It brought memories of failure with Pat. Then he remembered his wife for the first time since making love to Connie.

Immediate uneasiness slithered into his mind, squeezing at the joy they had shared, like some grossly perverted demon.

He started to say something to Connie, but couldn't find the words. What had happened could not be taken back. He had made love to Connie, regardless of all his arguments

154

and determination never to do so. And it had been love, passionate and total. That part of his life was over. He would have to face the results. He could only hope that Pat would never find out.

"I've got to go!" David said, starting to get up.

Connie grabbed at him. "No!"

That one word held all the demand and all the pleading a woman could put into a whole book of words.

Her hand touched his thigh and immediately he felt heated by the touch; She pulled him into her arms, smothering his lips with kisses. Her body trembled against his, her breasts soft, hot, like electricity driving through him.

All at once David didn't want to go anyplace. All he wanted was to possess Connie again. His nerves and body would not let him resist. Even his inner soul was screaming for her.

She urged him back against the bed, leaning over his form like some hungry goddess. Her eyes feasted on him, desire and wild erotic need burned there.

She wanted him as wantonly as he wanted her. It was like a fantastic energy that burst out from deep with them, gathering together into a cloud that enveloped the whole room with its fury.

David tried to pull away, tried to tell himself this was all wrong, that he had to get out of this woman's grip; get her out of his life, forever.

But the very power of their mutual need, their wild hunger was like a drug to an addict and he had doped his brain with it and was still helpless to resist. He had to have more.

She greedily grabbed at him. "There, love, that's what I want."

Then Connie leaned over, touched his chest with her lips, and ran her tongue down over his stomach, her hands gripping his thighs for support.

David felt uncontrolled wildness as he felt her tongue reach the tip of his now bursting hard. Then he was gripping her head, his fingers running through long silken hair as deep pleasure ripped at him like ocean waves brutally attacking a high cliff, beating savagely against the broken rocks of resis-

155

tance.

Then he was enveloped by voluptuous lips. Connie drove him to a teasing edge of ecstasy with the warmth of her moist mouth; held back, keeping him at the controlled peak until her kisses created anguished pinnacles of needle pain; she tugged wonderfully and erotically upon him, greedily attempting to draw the fiery wine of his bursting passions from their deeply hidden caves within his body. At the right moment, Connie's lips withdrew and then she recaptured him, her legs locking his body in place. Their bodies surged, merged and became one animal fire of passion, love and possession.

After that, David heard a voice screaming in the night; screaming and screaming in pleasure, until he didn't know if it was from overwhelming pleasure, pain or sick guilt.

He was unable to escape the joy and wonder of Connie, the woman who had captured his heart when it was still young and terribly innocent, and who had held him in her grasp all these years. And now would not let him go.

CHAPTER TWELVE

Pat woke from a horrid nightmare, shivering. The dream stayed with her only long enough to know it had been a nightmare concerning David leaving her. Then it slithered away. For a moment she couldn't place her surroundings; the room seemed oppressively dark. She sat up in bed, trying to clear her mind.

"Dave?" Her voice shook as she called to her husband. "Dave."

When no answer came to the more frantic call, Pat reached over to shake his shoulder. The bed was empty.

She turned on the lamp, fighting the disappointment about it being too early for David to be home. The whole night lay ahead of her, and that might mean more haunting dreams that could terrify her sleep, only to be washed away with returning consciousness.

As Pat saw the clock on the night stand beside the bed, panic laced little cruel fingers slowly clawing through her whole nervous system. The first reaction was to convince herself the clock must be fast.

She slipped out of bed, checked the plug. Everything was in order. She went to the clock-radio across the room.

It read the same time: 4:32.

"David!" she called, leaving the bedroom.

He might have slept in the den, rather than disturb her, Pat argued with herself.

As she stepped into the darkened den, the illusion of form shaped itself on the sofa, but as she moved nearer it turned out to be empty.

"David?" she called in a strained voice, again trying to convince herself that the panic was foolish, just an after-

157

math of the dream.

Moving to the front hallway, she stopped at the window to look across the neatly trimmed lawn to the driveway, where David always parked his car. Pat kept trying to tell herself there was no need for alarm. His car would be outside there, and he was somewhere in the house. Maybe in Eddie's room. But she had already searched most of the house. Connie's room and Eddie's were the only ones left.

Pat turned away from the window, trying to tell herself that it didn't matter that the car wasn't there. David would be all right.

She considered an auto accident with sudden new fear.

Then told herself David was a good driver, and decided against calling the police.

Pat found herself standing in front of the guest room, frightened in a new way. It was some time before she could label this new fear, and when realization came, her mind rebelled against it.

Connie was gone; hadn't come back after two nights.

David wasn't home. He had never been so late from a business appointment without calling her— and even then *never* this late!

Pat found herself visualizing David and Connie together in some cheap hotel room. He had probably never had a business appointment; it was probably all a lie to make it possible for the two of them to be together.

Sick inside, she realized how stupid she had been. Connie was a woman who had changed a lot, on the edge, very needy, and she and David had been very special that one summer so long ago. Apparently far more special than Pat had ever guessed. Or dared to admit.

Sick, Pat found herself behind the bar, holding a bottle of whiskey. She almost dropped the bottle, as if it were made of hot lead.

Her mind screamed over and over two names, hating both of them with such violence that she became frightened of herself.

David was the father of her child, the man she had married for better or for worse. But worse was not supposed

158

to mean something like this. *Worse* was supposed to be meanness, sickness, good and bad times. But infidelity, that was something else! And with her sister!

Pat's thoughts retracted her last point of reasoning. Many women had faced such a situation—maybe not with their sister being involved—but it boiled down to the same point. How had they handled it? That depended on what kind of person they were, how much they loved their husband; and how deep the hurt.

Getting up, she rejected the whole idea as crazy. David wouldn't do such a thing! You couldn't live with a man over a period of years without knowing what made him tick. He simply wasn't the kind of man who would cheat on her. Oh, flirt, like with Ruth the other night, even make a foolish pass under the influence of a drink but certainly not really cheat; not really take a woman in his arms and make love to her body.

Of course, in the past months the strain of his job, her own emotional insecurity about showing signs of aging, David's occasional failure in bed, could just possibly cause a man to enter into a situation that might normally never tempt him. And, she had to admit, Connie was certainly a temptation; a great one to David! If there was ever a woman who might threaten her marriage it was Connie.

"No," Pat told herself stubbornly. Trying to deny what she feared most. For she had never been able to compete with Connie. Few women could.

She was standing over the phone, and suddenly picked it up, determined to call the police and check if there had been any auto accidents that night.

* * * * * * *

David came out of the stupor as the morning sky was beginning to streak across the eastern horizon. For a moment he could not remember where he was; or what had happened last. Then memory slammed down like the blast of a rocket, almost crippling in its impact.

He jerked up in bed, not even turning to see Connie sleeping beside him. The last thing he remembered was the

159

frantic greed of Connie's body churning at him like a demon who couldn't torture a man enough. She had been greedy with passion. Consciousness had faded out after the final strength drained away.

The full implications of what had happened set in; and David was disgusted with himself, lost, unable to even think out the possible solutions. Connie had managed to mess up his life to the point where it would probably be impossible to piece it back together again in the same form it had been. He might have made things look good if he had called Pat—or gone home early enough. Now Pat could never forgive him for having done this—and she would surely guess the truth. With another woman—with Freda Hendricks—she might have been able to forget; in time. But with Connie, it was a far more complex situation, far more personal.

He moaned and slipped out of bed, going to the bathroom. His head was splitting; his mouth felt like a whole desert had been slammed into it. But that was the least of the problems. When he returned, Connie was sitting up in bed, her breasts uncovered, naked and beautiful above the sheets.

"What's wrong, Dave?" she asked in such an innocent voice that it might be possible to believe she did not really know and understand.

"Come off it," David retorted, looking at the window, wanting to run and hide, but knowing there was no escape from his own conscience. Even if he were able to convince Pat that he had stayed out on the business appointment all night, he would know the truth. But that possibility was out of the question, in any case, because he would have called her to let her know, so she wouldn't worry.

David went to the motel phone, picked it up, determined to call Pat and at least let her know that he was all right.

"What are you doing, Dave?" Connie cried, alarmed.

"Pat will be worried."

"Don't be a bloody fool! You call her now and everything will be ruined!"

David turned, looked at Connie, amazed. "Everything *is* ruined, already! And don't tell me you don't realize that!"

160

Connie laughed. It sounded harsh, mocking

"Oh, Dave, you are the silly one. Pat need never know the truth, if you only play it right. Believe me, I've heard every argument in the books, given by masters of the art of infidelity. Those guys in Hollywood know every trick in the trade. Like one guy told me, a wife will take any excuse to believe that her husband has *not* been cheating! He has everything in his favor, because a woman would rather fool herself than face the truth. You don't think Pat's any different, do you?"

"She'll know," David announced simply.

"The hell she'll know! Not unless you tell her. And you'd be a bloody fool to do that. We got something good going here. She never has to find out, until we decide just how far we want to take things."

She hesitated, looked down at the blanket, then added: "Last night...when you first arrived, and before that, for that matter, I figured it would be simple. Just let you make love to me, and then we'd tell Pat and leave town together. But I know now that it's more complicated than that, isn't it?" She looked up, her eyes wide, probing, almost honest.

"It's damned to hell more complicated!" David spat out. "It's over between the two of us, Connie. I only hope it won't be over between Pat and me."

Connie sounded alarmed as she cried: "What're you talking about?"

"Look, what happened last night, well, happened...well, just because it happened!" He felt lost for an explanation because suddenly he realized that it had not changed a thing about his feelings for Pat. Strangely enough he was not really too surprised about that.

"Now, come on, Dave, stop fooling yourself. You love me; and you know it. You've always loved me. That's why you married Pat. Don't be a bloody fool! Any second grade head-doc could figure that one out. You've *always* been *mine!*"

As she spoke, Connie slipped out of bed and moved to him. She now slid her arms around his neck, pressed her naked body close.

161

"Dave, you know I'm right. It was good between us—always was—but now better than ever before. Doesn't that prove something?" She appealed to him with her eyes, so innocent and wide, loving. "You said you loved me, Dave—remember? Last night you said you loved me."

David felt cold inside. "That was last night. This is morning."

"Morning doesn't change things between two people like us, Dave." She attempted to kiss him, but he forced her away, at arm's distance.

"Connie, I don't want to hurt you. I do love you, in my way I have always loved you and always will—but it isn't the same thing. I love Pat, too. And that love is more important, more meaningful. What our marriage has developed between us, the years of living experience, of being together, sharing the joy and the pains, and there's a lot of them, too...well that's different. What you and I have had, right from the beginning, was passionate desire, overwhelming joy of discovery, a wonderful, stunning summer of love. That can never be changed. Nor the feelings we share, a very special thing...but me and Pat have something else. Eddy for one thing. And all those years as a couple. We've been a success. I just hope we can somehow survive all this! This disaster!"

David was amazed by his own words. Last night it would have been impossible to have realized this truth; or said it to Connie.

She stared at him as if not quite understanding his words.

"Connie, don't you realize the truth. You should. You were the first one to point it out. Years ago you said something like sexual desire not being love. It was a long time ago; and you were very young. Now I realize, very wise, too!"

She laughed at that, it was a harsh, cutting sound that reverberated around the room like something live.

"You fool. I just had the hots for you. I couldn't wait to get the big man of mine giving it to me. It was simple sexual desire that made me say those words. There wasn't anything more to them than that. A reason to push you into mak-

162

ing love to me. I wanted to know you as a man—at least *that,* before I went to Hollywood. It was a hard decision to turn down your offer of marriage, *even then!* I needed a romance, complete with all the trimmings. I would have wanted it, in any case, even if I'd planned on marrying you, because I had read or heard somewhere that a man and woman should get to know one another before tying the marriage ropes around their necks—sorta to find if they suited one another sexually—to discover if it was nothing other than sexual need."

She attempted to move close. "It's different, now, Dave. I'm a woman, mature, experienced in life and love and I know we are right for each other. There was never a man like you, Dave. That's why my marriage was a failure, why any marriage with another man would be a shattering bore. You're the only man for me, Dave. You know that. We've been too much to each other for too long."

David held her off, away from him. "Connie, you might believe that, I don't know. But I'll tell you the truth. You meant a lot to me when I was young, because you were the first real love affair, the first girl I wanted to marry. I was young, had little experience with women. I didn't know the difference between sexual desire and real love. Maybe a man never really does know the difference until he's lived with a woman for a few years. It takes time, understanding, a lot of fights and living before a man and woman know what real love is all about. At first there's the sex angle. Afterwards, well, there's the emotional thing, the sharing of two lives together, the hardships, the joys, the holidays, the sicknesses, the learning that one is not alone and that there is somebody to share the pain and the pleasures of everyday living— somebody always there who cares if you live or die; or are happy or sick of living. The understanding shared between two people living years together is something far more important than sex. And all that fuses the relationship into something beyond jeweled gold. It was what makes us whole in a new sense of the word!"

"Now don't tell me sex is unimportant," Connie taunted with a bitter laugh. "Not after last night!"

"It has its place, yes."

"And surely you wouldn't have come here, Dave, if

163

your sex-life with Pat was good—if you were as truly happy with her as you try to let on."

"That's the mistake women make, Connie. There are other reasons for a man to be tempted into such a thing as happened last night. And it has nothing to do with his desire for his wife; or her ability to completely satisfy him. Maybe you don't know it, but with the woman you love, sex is good no matter what the end results. It becomes something more than mere physical release—it becomes an emotional thing. Maybe I had to be reminded of that. What happened here was not sharing or giving; but *taking!* With Pat it is giving with all my heart. You see, Connie, I married Pat because I fell in love with her—and for no other reason."

Connie stepped away from David, her face contorted in awful anguish. The emotion that whipped across her features changed from hurt to anger, then, in the last, dazed defeat. She collapsed down on the edge of the bed, looked up at him, eyes glazed, distant, hands clutched on her lap.

"Connie, please try to understand. I didn't know for sure until now. Last night I was emotionally all worked up over many things. If it's any help, what happened meant more to me than anything else in my life. But the reasons are totally different than you might guess."

"You really mean it?" Connie questioned in a flat voice. "You *really* love Pat."

"And all the more because of last night. It taught me the difference between sexual desire, even sexual love, and meaningful love. And..." he hesitated before continuing, "that there is a right place for sex in marriage. It isn't *everything*, even if important! The other things count more; and Pat knew this. I didn't really understand it fully until this morning."

David picked up the phone. "I won't be able to lie to Pat, Connie. I wish to God it were possible. I can only pray she'll understand and forgive."

"And if she doesn't?" Connie snapped, nastily.

"Well, I'll face that when the time comes. But it won't change things between you and me."

"No...I guess it won't, David," Connie announced, once more apparently in control of herself. She looked sud-

164

denly older, worn out by life, tired. "I guess I'll have to go back to Hollywood—or wherever life leads me."

"That would be best."

The motel operator answered the phone and David gave his home number. As he was waiting, he said to Connie: "I wish it was different for you, Connie."

"Don't bother! I made my own bed, so to speak, and now I'll rot in it." She took a cigarette from her purse. The actions of putting it in her mouth made her appear hard, cold. "I'll manage to survive. I always have. I learned the hard way! You better believe that!"

"Life can offer so much for a beautiful woman, Connie, if she merely looks with open eyes and—"

He broke off as Pat's voice sounded in the receiver. "Pat, Dave."

"Oh, God, where have you been?" she fairly screamed through the receiver. "I've been sick, out of my mind with worry and calling the police and—"

"Pat, darling, I love you more than you'll ever know."

"What's wrong?" she sounded alarmed, edgy, and suspicious.

"Nothing, any more. I've been a damned fool and I only hope you'll forgive me and understand." The words were popping out of his mouth like emotional tears from a baby; he couldn't stop them. "All I know is that I love you more than anything in the world and nothing can ever come between that love...if you'll have me."

Pat said, coldly, "Is Connie with you?"

Without hesitation David answered: "Yes. She's here."

"Oh," was the only thing that came over the receiver.

"Pat...darling, please let me explain and—"

"Go to hell, David. Just go to hell and leave me alone!"

The receiver went dead.

For a long time he stood there, numb, feeling as if somebody had brutally slammed him in the groin.

Connie's voice mocked the silence: "I told you, Dave. I told you not to be a damned bloody fool. Now what

165

are you going to do?"

She was standing in front of him, still naked, triumph marking every beautiful feature on her face. "Now it's just you and me, Dave. Just you and me."

"No, never you. Just get the hell out of my life," he told her in a flat dead voice. "Don't bother to do anything. Don't touch me. Don't speak to me. And don't ever let me see you again."

"David, you are out of your mind!" Connie cried, her voice high pitched. "It's us, now. You're free. Completely free. We'll get married as soon as you can get a divorce and—"

"Oh shut up, Connie. Just shut up. I wouldn't marry you if you were the last woman in the world. It's over. Flat over! All you are to me is...well, nothing better than a one-night stand. I should have known the truth from the beginning I'm sorry about that. All I wanted from you was...well, I had to find out the truth. I was just too damned stupid to know it without sleeping with you. Okay, you got what you wanted. You broke it with Pat and me—you screwed me! Okay, leave it there. But the prize is denied all of us. We're all finished. I made the mistake of thinking a woman could forgive me. But...I guess I simply went too far. Pat is a human being, a very tender, sensitive female—and God knows how I've hurt her. It's too late to make it up to Pat. It's too late for everything. So just leave me alone...or so help me, I'll kill you!"

David turned away and started gathering up his clothes. He dressed in a daze and then opened the motel door. Without turning back, he closed the door behind him and walked to his car.

He felt nothing other than regret for what had happened. He didn't even blame Pat. Probably no woman in the world would forgive a husband for sleeping with her own sister. He should have realized that and not been so weak. His own selfish longing for forgiveness had driven him to push Pat *too* far. If only he could have told her a lie, if only he could have tried to give her a way out. Room to save face. She might guess the truth, but her pride wouldn't have been stripped naked and brutally beaten beyond recovery.

166

A choking sob broke from his lips as he slipped behind the wheel of his car. His mind roared over and over: *How could I have hurt Pat so much?*

He felt cheap, sick and disgusted with himself. Everything in him cried to go to Pat and help her, make her understand, to take the pain away, no matter what it cost him.

Then he would go out of her life; if that's what she wanted; knowing he had lost the most wonderful woman in the world; for pure selfish stupidity

As David gunned the car out of the parking lot, his thoughts shifted, directed themselves along the road of easy escape, total escape from everything. It would be so easy to drive the car into a fatal accident. Then he wouldn't have to think about what he had done to Pat; he wouldn't have to live with himself for the rest of his natural life, knowing the pain he had caused. Death was a simple, easy answer.

And never to see Eddy again. Even as a divorced father.

David's right foot pressed the gas pedal to the floor and kept it there as the car shot down the highway, gaining speed faster and faster, screaming around the curves, shooting recklessly past the oak trees that lined the road on both sides. Then suddenly at a sharp curve he couldn't correct the car's course, a huge tree loomed ahead like a greedy shadow leaping up from Hell's pits to claim him.

Frantically, David attempted to avoid collision, aware too late that death was coward's way out and not a solution.

At the last moment he pulled the car to the right, sighed out his relief as it appeared he'd escaped; then suddenly the world exploded in a series of sparks, his ribs slammed against the steering wheel, his head struck the windshield and blackness descended like the hand of death.

* * * * * * *

It took Connie a long time to get control of her emotions after David walked out of the motel room. She lay on the bed, sobbing uncontrollably. The world seemed to have closed her out. She didn't belong in her family's life; childhood friends would never be more than memories—off-

167

limits; like the town in which she was raised and matured into a starry-eyed young girl wanting Hollywood and the Big City. Suddenly Small Town, USA—all of them—seemed welcomed heavens from the cold impersonal world of the metropolitans.

After she accepted the fact that David was not coming back, that she was completely off his list, Connie felt another reaction slowly eat its way through her being and mind.

Everything had been for nothing. She was right back where she had started, except with the knowledge that David would never be hers. Maybe, in a sense, that was a gain. She didn't know, yet.

With that realization, Connie wondered if it really mattered. It had been so good with him, but could they have ever been happy together? David was different than she remembered him. As a young man he would never have turned her down. As a man in his thirties he had done exactly that, as if she had been nothing more than a cheap thrill, a whore to bed down with for the night.

And suddenly that's the way Connie felt. It was the way she had acted with the pick-up the other night. She had gone after David, a married man in love with his wife, like a tramp, hotly trying to tempt him from a happy home.

All at once Connie began seeing exactly what she had done to her sister and David and wished it could all be taken back, now that she knew there was no way to win him for herself.

Maybe she had been looking for something that was a part of her youth and childhood, trying to recapture the past, so that the present could be wiped out? It fit. She should have known that nobody can go back. Once an event took place it marked you like a scar on your face. One had to learn to live for the present, and make the best of what life offered.

It took time for the realization to set in fully. But in the end, Connie knew she had to do something to make amends, to put the pieces back together before she left for Hollywood. She couldn't leave David and Pat on the verge of a divorce, all because of what she had forced David into. Then, if things worked out right, maybe the Big City would

168

have some kind of happiness for her; now that she could accept David as part of her lost youth and past.

After all, nobody made it big is show-biz or life without fighting to the bitter end. Succeed, one way or the other, until death crushed all possible choices. Nobody made it over night, it took time, effort and blind determination. Maybe she'd given up too soon in Hollywood. Maybe it was time to return and fight some more.

But first she had to make things right between her sister and David. If it wasn't too late.

Connie gathered her things and checked out of the motel. Some twenty minutes later she drove up in front of Pat's small house on the outskirts of town.

* * * * * * *

Pat heard the front door open, but paid no attention. She simply sat in the living room chair, staring at the wall, unmoving, like she had done for the last hours. Time had shattered, drifted off into loose disconnected pieces ever since talking to David. If only he had tried to lie, anything— just given her a way out. They could have lived through the next awkward weeks, and after a while the hurt would have numbed over, maybe even died.

"Pat," came a soft voice in front of her.

It was some moments before she realized that Connie was standing directly in her line of vision. She hadn't noticed the other woman coming up.

"*Pat!* Snap out of it!"

She looked at her sister, feeling nothing.

"Pat...please. I'm leaving...I have to tell you something!" Connie sounded desperate.

Pat stared blankly at her. "There's nothing to say! You've done quite enough!"

"Pat...there's so much...you don't understand."

Sudden fury bit at Pat, she stood, her body tensed like a spring. Her fists doubled up. It was difficult to control the urge to strike out physically at Connie.

"I understand you slept with Dave." Pat started to leave the room. "Screw you, you damned *whore!* You've

169

fucked him and my life…fucked it all away!"

"David loves you."

Connie came up from behind, grabbed her shoulder, and yanked her around. "I wanted him. I did everything I could do to get him back. He was mine before he was yours. I thought he still was mine. I was *wrong!* Don't you see? He loves you—and nothing I could do would shake that!"

Pat backed away, her face contorted. "You never were happy to leave things alone. You're like a sickness. Just get out of my house."

Connie blinked, then said: "I'm a human being. I've seen a lot of dirt in the world. You fight for what you want, winner take all. That's the way it is. If you don't have the guts to fight, you don't deserve the rewards. I tried not to do it, Pat, believe me. I wouldn't have, if I'd known the truth. I wouldn't have even come here if I had believed this would happen. I think maybe both David and myself had to find out the truth!"

Pat fought back the churning emotions. She had never hated with such violence. All she could think of was how their lives had been ruined by this woman who was now a total stranger.

"Just leave me alone, Connie. I don't want to ever see you again."

Connie laughed. "How ironic! That's what David said, after talking to you. He doesn't want to see me again, either. I guess I'm a total washout here."

"You don't belong, you never did," Suddenly Pat felt more calm. "You know, Connie, men desire women like you like they desire a whore. You're a sickness...a disease that should be cut out...or kept out of decent people's lives."

"Just back down, Pat! You live in a closed, small world, which is sheltered by men like Dave. You don't know the full meaning of the outside world—you've been protected all your life. So where do you get off telling me I'm sick. The whole damned rotten world is sick. That's the facts! And when a woman gets a man like Dave she's a fool to throw him aside just because he made one slip. What makes you so goddamn perfect? What makes you think you have the right to forgive or not forgive? You should count yourself lucky that Dave loves you and wants you above everybody else. You haven't a thing to worry about, ever— not with Dave. So stop feeling so damned sorry for yourself! What would you do if he dropped dead right now? How would you feel? Think about that, Pat. And be glad the two of you are alive. I'm leaving as soon as 1 get my things packed. But you have to stay here, and you can mess up your life completely or get smart."

Connie turned to move toward the guest room, then paused, faced Pat. "David's a fine man. You have something special. I wish to God I had him...I could have had him, years ago. I chickened and lost!"

Then she added as if an afterthought. "I tried to warn him not to tell you the truth. I said it would be better to lie than let you know. But he couldn't help himself. He *couldn't* lie! That's a rare thing. Most husbands do lie. Most lie through their teeth every time they speak to their wives. And nobody is the wiser. At least you'll always know exactly where you stand with him—if you are wise enough to not let this ruin your marriage."

With that, Connie left the room.

Pat went into the den, fixed herself a drink, sat on the barstool, sipping the liquor. She listened to Connie's words over and over again in her mind, trying to feel something. But she felt emotionally blank. The shock of learning the brutal truth was just too much.

She finished off the drink, then heard the door to Connie's room open, followed by footsteps.

"Pat, I'm sorry," Connie's voice said from the door- way. "I hope that someday we can forget all this. It was beastly of me...I just happened to love the same man you do. That's *all*. Good-bye. I'll—"

The phone rang, breaking into her words.

Pat ignored it.

When it continued, Connie said: "I'll get it."

Pat hardly heard the sudden cry of alarm from Con- nie.

A moment later, Connie was shaking her.

"It's Dave," Connie cried, high pitched, frightened. "Pat...Dave's been in an accident."

171

She merely stared at the wall, without really hearing her sister's voice.

Suddenly something struck her face. Pat felt the stinging blow, and for a brief instant, she didn't understand what had happened. Then Connie slapped her again.

Tears welled in Pat's eyes.

"Pat—for God's sake. It's the hospital. Dave's been in an auto accident!" Connie yelled, shaking Pat like a dog shaking a rag.

The tears streamed down Pat's cheeks. She sobbed slightly, and felt suddenly dizzy.

"Pat, he *needs* you! Don't be a fool. He'll need you! Don't you *understand?*" Connie cried. "There's been an accident. He's on the critical list. You *have* to go to him...now! Please, Pat..."

Pat said nothing. She tried to understand what Connie was telling her; tried to react emotionally to it, but couldn't do anything but sit there sobbing.

"Pat...listen...you have—"

"Leave...me...alone!"

"Pat, either you go to Dave right now or I'm *going!*" Connie announced in a determined voice, stepping away. "He's going to need somebody—and it'll either be you there or me!"

* * * * * * *

It was like coming out of a dream world, a distant darkness which surged around him, that flinted away, then folded back into being, without form or sound.

He lived in this darkness, aware, but unable to think. It was as if everything were disconnected—the plugs pulled out. How long it lasted, David could not determine. It was an endless void, both in time and space.

Yet consciousness slowly became more alive, information trickling in like sand drifting down to the bottom half of an hour glass. He remembered his early years of high school and the face of a young, pretty girl, which kept shifting, aging, and then changing shape. At first he could not pinpoint a name to go with the face. Then just as he was on

172

the verge of thinking the name Connie, another name flashed into being:

Pat.

And both names fit the changing face.

With sharp awareness the last pieces of information slammed into being and David heard a muffled scream.

He remembered the accident, remembered what had happened between Connie and himself—and what it had done to his marriage.

He had been trying to escape the pressures of the present-day world, to forget, for a moment, what was attempting to crush in at his life. The sexual failures with Pat now seemed to have been mentally blown up far out of importance. It hadn't been much more than embarrassing with Connie—and he readily accepted her assurance that it didn't matter. With Pat, he had loved her so much, wanted to give so much pleasure, that in his mind the failures were multiplied in importance. With Connie he had continued trying—partly because he had rode along with the sensual games they played. With Pat he had given up in frustration and guilt, allowing himself the luxury of self-pity—and thereby believed it was useless to continue trying until success proved the event of little importance. Then the fear and inner guilt had eaten at his subconscious, stagnating there, rotting until an infested emotional sore took control of all logic.

But, David now knew, he had learned something else, far more important. Sex itself was not the full-scope of married life, and relations with another woman whom he did not truly love, was only half the thing it was with Pat. There was far more to their marriage than successful sexual relations. There was emotional love. Their lives were a blend of understanding and love, which had become as much a part of him as his arms and legs. Without Pat, he would be thrust onto an endless, hostile ocean, without the will or strength to even seek out survival.

Then...

David became aware of a distant sound, of lying on his back in bed. His chest hurt, but everything was vague—even the pain.

The only thing in real focus was his mental need for

173

Pat. Even if he lost his job they'd survive, somehow. Even if they had to sell their home and go live in an apartment—the only thing that mattered to him was Pat and Eddie—he'd been too blind with self-pity to understand that until now.

Now that it was too late.

He moaned and knew it was his own voice that had screamed a short time before.

"He's regaining consciousness," a low, far-away voice announced.

He tried to open his eyes, but they were like lead. His mouth felt terribly dry, his head was beginning to throb. The pain in his chest grew from dull ache to a crushing band running all the way around his upper body.

A soft voice sounded from his left, but he couldn't make out the words.

David tried to turn his head, but couldn't move. Panic set in, then he wanted to scream, but couldn't make his throat move.

Something soft, warm, touched his face, and then patted his hand. Small, delicate fingers were holding him, caressing.

The male voice said: "I wouldn't stay with him too long. He's had a long struggle. Okay?"

Images formed in front of his eyes, but then faded. He had a vague memory of speaking to some woman, but couldn't be sure who it was. Black settled down on him, then flashed away as full consciousness returned.

He was lying in bed, sweating, his chest hurt, and the pain on his right temple felt like a knife had cut the flesh. But it mattered little.

Sunlight was beaming from a window across his eyes.

David rang for a nurse. Then waited.

He looked around him, moving with painful care. There were several bowls of flowers around the room.

When the nurse came, he asked: "Where did all this come from?" He indicated the flowers.

The nurse smiled. "Well, that's original. Usually they ask 'where am I?'"

She went through automatic motions of taking his

174

pulse, then shoved a thermometer into his mouth.

"Maybe you'd like to read the cards," she offered, taking a few tiny envelopes from the stand next to the bed. "There's someone wanting to see you."

David didn't have time to ask who before the nurse had left the room.

Automatically he looked at the envelopes. One was from the office, he was sure. He opened it.

"We're all waiting your return. Congratulations on the contract and promotion. Get well fast. Nathan will be needing some help from his new assistant office manager. Best, Harvey."

He opened another without emotion. *"Well, you were a good combatant; I guess you'll be a good fighter against the hospital. My best wishes, Freda."*

David tried to feel something, but there wasn't anything within him that could respond to the notes. It was all meaningless without Pat.

The nurse returned and took the thermometer from his mouth.

David was about to say something when he heard a high-pitched little voice cry out:

"Daddy."

A small, blonde-haired boy with freckles approached the bedside. Arms clung around David's neck.

"Be careful, young man!" the nurse warned, stepping back. "You know you aren't supposed to be here."

For a moment David couldn't say anything. He just wondered where the hell Eddie had come from.

"You're supposed to be in camp," he managed in a choked voice.

"Daddy, Daddy, we've been worried." His son looked up into his eyes, tears beginning to stream down those puffy red cheeks.

"What's there to worry about? You know nothing can happen to your Daddy."

Then David saw a taller, willowy form behind his son, standing just a few feet away.

"Pat," he cried, unable to control the moisture in his own eyes.

What could he tell her? How would he ever make her understand how sorry he was?

"Hello, Dave," she said, as the nurse took Eddie in hand, gently leading him out of the room.

"Pat...can you ever—"

She cut him short with:

"Just shut up and listen to me!" Then she tenderly took his hand in hers. "I got myself a good husband! Everybody can make one mistake. Just don't you ever try doing something like that again. You hear?" she scolded, with a mocking frown on her lovely face.

"Believe me, honey—"

But her soft, warm lips cut him short as they covered his.

David had seen tears in her lovely eyes and knew he had the most wonderful woman in the world. What was more, he would never look any further than Pat, never as long as he lived.